THE STARVING DETECTIVES

FROM THE FILES OF THE SOFT BOILED DETECTIVE AGENCY

TOM MCGRAW

Cover Illustration by
AVA PRISK

*This book is dedicated to my children and wife.
In particular to my father who always, always
encouraged my writing, even when it was
unfit to wrap fish in. I'm sorry you never got
to see this in print. I miss you Dad.*

*The author can be contacted at
tommcgraw@outlook.com*

Set Books Publishers 2017

Copyright 2016

CONTENTS

NATHAN KAVILLEHOGG BURNS HIS
PIGGIES MAKING NACHOS

NATHAN KAVILLEHOGG SAT at his desk in his parent's backyard shed. It *was* a fairly large and useful shed before Nathan commandeered it. Now crammed in it was a 1970s-era government desk, a huge thing that barely allowed Nathan to shimmy behind it.

The remaining space was packed with his father's tools. Many of these hung from stout hooks in the ceiling. Hedge trimmers, house jacks, and miter saws; all seemed to defy gravity floating above and around his desk when one entered the shed. This tended to make first-time visitors vaguely nauseous or feel somewhat off-kilter. This happened infrequently, however. Never, to be blunt, as no one had come to him with a case to be solved.

Twisting uncomfortably in his chair, Nathan began wrestling with the tiny microwave directly behind him which was wedged between the belt sander and a truly impressive iron vise. He just managed to get the bowl of nacho cheese dip out and around without spilling it. He did not, however, escape burning the stew out of his fingertips. Half-dropping the bowl on his desk, he stuffed his burned piggies in his mouth. Swiveling in his chair, he pulled the bottom drawer of his filing cabinet out with his foot. Using both feet in a crab-like pincer motion, he tossed up a bag of tortilla chips onto his desk knocking over the steaming orange goop.

"Ah, man!" he muttered as the steaming magma-like substance ate into the steel surface of his desk.

Scooping it off the desktop with a tortilla chip and cramming it into his mouth, he settled down to the business of *eating* the nachos when the door was wrenched wide open.

ENTER JERICHO KAVILLEHOGG

JERICHO KAVILLEHOGG BURST into the shed.

"Hah! Eating! Sticky nachos, no less!" Jericho belted out. His way of speaking, like his manner, was larger than life. Jericho himself was big, scary big, in a way that wienie dogs aren't. His shoulders filled the wide doorway.

Most men would be frightened at this sight, but Nathan only felt dread. Not for his own physical safety, but for that of his snack, as he now *knew* he would never get to eat his tortilla chips.

"This is for your own good Nathan!" Jericho barked as he lunged for the steaming cheese and corn chips.

"Thank God for Mexico!" Jericho managed to say as he shoved handfuls of chips into his mouth. He breathed in sharply, stopped, and coughed, spraying Nathan with wet flecks of tortilla. Jericho jerked his face up and explosively coughed again, lodging a wad of cheesy chips onto an overhanging rototiller attachment.

"Gosh Jericho," Nathan managed through pursed lips as he brushed chips off his shoulders.

Jericho lurched forward and grabbed another handful of chips, destroying more than he was getting.

"Little brother, *I love these things!*" Jericho sputtered, his mouth full. Nathan looked about as if the walls were about to cave in on them. Jericho darted his eyes over the cluttered desktop, stopping on an open can of Sugar Bomb cola. The brothers locked eyes for a moment. Both lunged for the can.

"Mine!" Nathan squeaked as Jericho grabbed the can first.

"Sorry little brother, but this must be washed down!" he said and upended the can, crushing it to force the soda down his gullet faster than gravity could limply manage on its own. The result was dramatic in the confined space of the shed. Soda fanned around Jericho's head in an arc, soaking everything.

"AHHHHH!" Jericho burbled, slamming the

empty can on the steel desktop, crumpling it into a
hockey puck and causing everything to jump seven
and a half inches into the air. He proceeded to
punch himself in the gut causing a mammoth belch
to leap from his hard belly. With a wide sweep of his
arm, he cleared a spot on Nathan's sticky, chip-
encrusted desk.

"Tell me about business little bro!"

Nathan composed himself and said, "Dad and,
I'm certain, Mom wants me to start paying rent and
whatnot." Nathan finished the job of wiping chip
crumbs and splatters of cola off his desk.

"Yeah, that's a bummer, but it's time you did. You
gotta get out there and grab a client! With both
hands! Like this!" Jericho bellowed as he seized
Nathan, picked him up, and began to shake him like
a scary and rickety roller coaster ride. Jericho grew
tired of this after a few minutes and set the now limp
Nathan behind the old steel desk. Nathan raised his
head and looked at Jericho who was now strumming
his abs with his muscular fingers.

"Gosh Jericho, I wish I had your self-esteem. I
seem to have trouble enough with eating a bowl of
cereal in the morning," Nathan mumbled.

"What do you mean, self-esteem?" said Jericho
and eyed Nathan warily.

"Well, you know, how you view yourself as great and all."

Jericho stopped messing with his abs for a moment and creased his brow.

"But I am great," he said, confused.

"See what I'm talking about?" Nathan said.

"Women tell me that all the time, hell, men too! The sky's blue Nathan, why are you telling me what everyone knows?" Jericho paused and picked up a thick steel T-square and started to twist it into a spring shape.

"Hey! Dad's going to think I did that!" Nathan said and gawked at the ruined tool.

Jericho looked at the DNA-shaped ruler and laughed, "Naw man, he's not gonna think that!" He smiled broadly and hurled it into the cement floor where it sparked from the force of the impact. It quivered, bolt upright, embedded at least three inches into the floor. He reached over the desk and jabbed Nathan in the shoulder.

"Let's grab a drink!" Jericho said as he pulled Nathan into a standing position.

"Umm, I don't really *want* a drink," Nathan almost whispered.

"WHAT!? You're a detective! You're a Kavillehogg!" Jericho brayed as he pushed Nathan out of the shed into the crazy-bright sunlight. Nathan squinted.

Jericho turned his own face to the sun, and with his fingers, wrenched opened his own eyes as wide as they would go.

"Come on Sun! Is that the best you got!?" Jericho yelled as he shook both fists at the great ball of fire in the sky.

JOE'S CUP OF JOE

ON THE BAR top of the coffee dive called Joe's Cup of Joe, Nathan drummed his fingers. Excited, he turned to Jericho and said, "Do you realize in the novel Moby Dick, Captain Ahab said 'I would strike the sun if it offended me?'"

"Look man, this is a workin' man's coffee shop, alright? Don't be talkin' about books of any kind, like not even an atlas, okay?" Jericho said quietly, looking about. "That would start a fight even *I* couldn't get us out of."

"Oh, yes, sorry," said Nathan.

A huge guffaw tore itself loose from Jericho. He slapped Nathan on the back almost knocking him off his chair.

"I'm jokin' man. I could beat up an Indian

Elephant. Really — like this!" Jericho punched the edge of the bar, splintering the wood and causing all the drinks to slosh. He then grabbed a sugar decanter and poured a good fifteen tablespoons worth into his coffee causing his spoon to stand upright in his mug.

A tired-looking man slowly turned to Nathan and said meekly, "Drinking java is supposed to be a relaxing thing. When your friend comes in, it well, puts my teeth on edge."

"Jericho's kind of like a glacier," Nathan said tiredly. "It's impossible to stop him from doing anything."

The coffee barfly nodded and slowly turned back to his drink.

Jericho grabbed his own head, jerked it hard to the left, popped his neck, and bellowed, "This latte stuff is making me tired, let's switch to espresso shots!"

THE SHED IS ON FIRE!

SEVERAL HOURS later Nathan was back at his desk. His brother Jericho was in the far corner on the riding lawn mower, face down across the steering wheel, unconscious, possibly from diabetic shock. Nathan wrestled with a snack-size bag of So Spicy It'll Make Ya Blind brand potato chips. Initially tugging at the top he gave up and began to squeeze it from the bottom. Squeezing too hard the bag burst open erupting chips into the air like a junk food volcano. Startled, he looked up, allowing several of the zesty chips to fall onto his gaping eyes. The high-potency spices and salt did their work. He leapt from the office chair and caught both kneecaps on the edge of the heavy desk.

"AGHHHH! I'M BLIND!" he yelled, startling

Jericho awake. From his half-sleeping, sugar-comatose stupor, Jericho wrenched himself up. He managed to catch his foot in the steering wheel and landed face down on the desk and into the spicy potato chip landmines. The effect was galvanizing.

"AGHHHH! I'M BLIND TOO!" Jericho bellowed into his brother's face.

"DON'T TOUCH YOUR EYES!" Nathan said as he smacked right into a hanging miter saw.

"WHAAA? WHY NOT?!" Jericho said and immediately rubbed his eyes. He jerked bolt upright onto his heels and stumbled about, like Frankenstein's Monster. "AGHHHH! IT BURNS LIKE ACID!" Jericho babbled, and rubbed harder. He blundered into a dangling fishing net. "I'M CAUGHT IN A SPIDER'S WEB!" he blubbered.

Behind them, the shed door was opened, flooding the dark tool shed with blazing light. The brothers spun to the hot glaring light, fear showing on their greasy, potato chip-smeared faces.

"AGHHH! THE SHED'S ON FIRE!" they screamed in unison.

ENTER THE FEMME FATALE

"NO, IT'S NOT," a husky female voice said quietly.

Hearing a woman's voice caused Jericho to recover quickly.

"But of course it isn't," he said, directly to the mop bucket in the corner. The woman's hands firmly turned him to face in her direction. This caused a dandruff-like drift of broken potato chips to fall on her arms.

"WHERE ARE YOU?" shrieked Nathan as he spun in circles, his arms pirouetting.

"Please stop panicking," said the calm woman.

"Kavillehoggs don't panic," Jericho said, blindly addressing her shoulder bag. "But my brother here does become — *excited*." He emphasized this as he wagged a finger at an empty space, as the woman uprighted a chair and sat down.

Nathan felt around for the desk and gingerly sat. "How can I help you?" he muttered to an old broken vacuum cleaner.

"Over here," she said.

"Ah, yes. Name?"

"Jacqueline Portsmouth."

Jericho turned and, reaching blindly about in the air, managed to jamb his pinky finger into her ear. "What the — oh, gosh!" he muttered.

Jacqueline dislodged the finger and, grabbing his forearm and sat him on the desktop facing a toolbox.

"Does your 'office' operate like this daily?"

"Not daily," Nathan whimpered. Jacqueline laughed, an easy soft sound. Nathan relaxed and felt around for a pen amongst the chip crumbs.

"I will leave you a card," she said. Then she dropped it in his hand and clasped his greasy spicy fingers around it. "Call me when you can see. I would like to meet at a pharmacy, if convenient."

Jericho straightened and arched an eyebrow, "Do you mean a drug store? Why?"

Jacqueline stood, straightened her skirt, and glancing at the two pathetic detectives said, "It's clean. And bright."

A PITIFUL VISIT TO THE PHARMACY

LATER, having regained their sight, Nathan and Jericho walked nimbly into Carl's Ginormous Pharmacy and sheepishly looked from one customer to the next.

"Man, it doesn't happen much, but I feel like a clod," Jericho tried to say quietly, which, for him was like a bellow coming from a normal person.

"What do you think she looks like, you know, by her voice?" Nathan said.

Jacqueline Portsmouth walked up behind them and tapped their shoulders at the same time. As if shocked by a car battery, Nathan jumped straight up. Jericho snapped into a grotesque parody of a karate stance.

"Holy Roman Emperor," she said. "Are you two for real?"

Standing in the Incontinence Aisle, Jacqueline stood straight, her hands on her hips. Nathan was turned slightly away from her, his head bowed down, looking as if he felt she would hit him with a rolled newspaper. Jericho, as are all hardheads with inflated self-worth, stood straight, chest puffed out as if he owned the world.

"My problem sounds fairly straightforward — but isn't," Jacqueline said quickly as if the matter were settled.

Jericho was fascinated by a package of adult diapers he had taken off the shelf. He raised his eyebrows and nodded slightly, agreeing with what he read.

Nathan, who was actually *listening* to their client, scrunched his eyebrows. He took a deep breath and tried to relax his furrowed brow. It didn't work.

"Could you be less — opaque?" Nathan said, not meeting her eyes. She came very close to him. He cringed and closed his eyes. Seeing this, Jacqueline backed up a step or two. Nathan relaxed visibly. Then she got closer and backed up several times, quickly. Nathan became a human accordion, collapsing and expanding.

Broken from his incontinence fantasy, Jericho raised the pack of diapers over her like a sledgehammer. Her head swiveled toward him and she hissed like a goose.

"High tailin' Jiminy!" he managed through a mask of terror, dropping the pack of diapers on his head. She suppressed a laugh and looked about.

Nathan was long gone.

"Be a detective and find your brother," she said turning, "what's up with you two?"

Jericho walked backward, not taking his eyes from her he managed through clenched teeth, "Our mother is a *very willful woman*!" He turned and scampered off to find his brother.

She watched the receding figure of the hunched-over man, his arms swinging like a baboon's. "Scared of women! Crazy people left and right," she said and smiled to herself. She returned the fallen adult diapers to the shelf and, as she strolled out, stopped and straightened every item which was even a little crooked.

THE CASE IS LAID BARE

NATHAN WAS SITTING outside the pharmacy his head between his knees. Standing beside him, Jericho was pulling at his own hair and making motorboat noises with his mouth.

"Man, I hate that!" Jericho said.

"It's *embarrassing!*" squeaked Nathan.

Grabbing Nathan's leg, Jericho raised his brother up using one hand and dusted his brother's pants off with the other as Nathan dangled upside down.

At this moment Jacqueline strode out through the USS Enterprise-like sliding doors. She glared at the two brothers.

"When you fear a foe, fear crushes your strength; and this weakness gives strength to your opponents," Jacqueline said, shaking her head.

This proper use of English momentarily made Jericho's brain freeze up, which caused him to drop his brother on his head. Nathan quickly fumbled upright and kneeled before her, blood dribbling out of his nose.

"Do you realize you're quoting Shakespeare?!" Nathan blurted out.

She raised one eyebrow.

Nathan scrambled to a kneeling position and meekly put out his hand. She shot hers out and wrung it hard. Nathan winced and tried to smile as blood trickled down from his nose and stained his teeth red.

"Whatever your issue, I'm confident we can devise a solution to your quandary," Nathan said.

She looked to Jericho who was squinting at them.

"You two talkin' Belgian?" he muttered.

Jacqueline ignored Jericho and focused on the detective kneeling before her.

"My father has disappeared and I need him found by nine a.m. tomorrow morning," she said.

Nathan clambered up, looked her straight in the eyes and said, "We will make this happen. I will tear up my detective's license if it doesn't."

Jericho twisted at his waist and looked down at the back of his own pants.

"What *are* you doing?" Jacqueline said.

"Thought I just soiled myself, but it was a false alarm," he said and nodded to himself, "Maybe I shoulda bought some of them *adult diapers*."

THE URGENCY OF THE CASE

ENTERING THE CROWDED SHED, Jacqueline glanced about and looked for a place to sit.

"Flummoxed," she said.

Jericho, behind her, smacked his head on a hanging seed spreader as he said, "What did you say?"

Nathan, wedged behind the massive desk raised a single finger. "To be flummoxed is to be confused, confounded, bewildered — "

"Buffaloed!" Jacqueline said, following with an impressively high-pitched laugh. So high, in fact, that Jericho's lower fillings hurt.

"Yes! Oh, that's perfect!" Nathan said.

"How often do you get to say that?!" Jacqueline said, her eyes glowing.

"Never!" they said in unison.

Jericho backed out through the rusty door, saying, "Look, I'm goin' to get a dictionary. The *big* one."

Nathan, clearly entranced by the woman, waved him off casually.

Jericho shrugged, turned, and walked straight into a hanging ice cooler.

"A seat?" Jacqueline said.

"Oh, I'm terribly sorry," Nathan said and, trying to get up from behind the desk too fast smashed his thighs under the unyielding desk and yelped.

Jacqueline swept some spicy chips off the desk and eased onto it.

"Yes, that's better," he said, placing his hands behind his head and leaned back on the chair until his head hit the wall.

Jacqueline was arranging the remaining spicy chips into a pattern. "You enjoy starchy, salty snack foods?" she said.

"Though I've never been in love, I would imagine it's something like corn chips and green onion dip..." he muttered, increasingly caught up in a junk food fantasia. He drifted off until he realized she was speaking to him, waving her hand in front of his now glassy eyes.

"Stay with me, Kavillehogg!" she said. "You have it bad, huh?"

"Yeah, it's more than just enjoyment, it's, it's, more like Brahma, a oneness with the universe, you know?" he said.

Arching an eyebrow she said, "Not with corn chips and dip I don't." She had finished arranging the corn chips in a model of daVinci's Golden Ratio.

"That's pretty cool," He said, picking out one of the chips and popping it in his mouth. "The DaVinci thing and all."

"Until you *ate it*. Those stale chips were on a dirty desk."

He quickly swept the chips onto the floor and cleared his throat.

"Now, about your father. Any details? In the business we call them *leads*," he said, nodding easily, like a sage.

"He was at a boat rental agency on the back bayou. He was —"

"Which one?"

"I hadn't finished my sentence."

"Oh, sorry!"

"It's understandable, this must be very exciting for you. He had rented a dual-hull pontoon boat to take —"

"Dual pontoon... oh, a *party barge*! I thought —"

"That you had interrupted me again, yes, you had. And incidentally, only beer-swilling thrill seekers, upon their dubious 'retirement,' use the term *party barge*. Marine researchers and the remainder of the planet's population use pontoon boats. If you cannot refrain from interrupting me, perhaps I should leave you to dust off your unused etiquette manual," she said and started to get up.

"Please. Sit. I am somewhat worked up, but only to get *cracking* as we say in the business. I promise I will not interrupt again," he said, crossed his fingers, and made a zipping motion across his lips.

"Did you just zip your lip!?" she said and delivered another of her high-pitched laughs, causing an empty glass to vibrate and form hair-thin cracks in it.

Nathan dropped his hand into his lap, mortified.

She sat and said, "He has not been seen since. Being terrified of bodies of water, he rarely travels on them, and never past nightfall."

A long moment passed.

She cleared her throat, leaned forward, and said, "Well?"

Nathan jerked his head back as if he had licked a nine-volt battery and said, "Oh, sorry, I was afraid, no, *cautious*, of not breaking your narrative. But, but, what was he doing on a boat if he — doesn't like the water?"

For the first time, her almost overbearing presence faltered. She didn't quite look Nathan in the eye as she said, "He was doing his job. He *is* the world's leading marine researcher."

Nathan licked some of the So Spicy It'll Make Ya Go Blind potato chip fragments off his palm and said confusedly, "But he's scared of the water."

"Not the water so much as being, well, *swallowed by a whale.* You see, he attended Catholic private schools, and the nuns, when not busy shaming him, told him if he didn't do as they said, he would, like Jonah, be swallowed by a whale," she said and straightened her back and showed her palms as if it was all clear now.

Nathan nodded knowingly and said, "That nun stuff sticks. In the business, we call that *messed up.*"

A MISGUIDED TRIP DOWN THE DRIVEWAY

THIRTY-SEVEN MINUTES LATER, in their parent's two-car garage, Jericho wrenched the transmission lever down, hard. This was followed by an awful, terrible grinding sound as if someone had thrown a toaster oven under a lawn mower. The avocado green, 1972 Land Barge station wagon lurched forward. Nathan gripped the captain's chair armrests very tightly so as to keep himself from fleeing the vehicle.

"Hey man, you're gonna tear up the armrests with your fingernails," Jericho said as the hideous station wagon lurched down the driveway. "I mean gosh, look what you're doing."

"Please focus on the somewhat forward motion

of this vehicle," Nathan said between clenched teeth. He glanced down and with effort, relaxed his grip, pulling some armrest stuffing out with his deeply entrenched fingernails. A brief smile appeared on his lips as he flexed his puny forearms.

Jericho saw this, barked out an explosive laugh, and said, "Welcome to the gun show!"

CRASH!!!

In his revelry, Jericho managed to smash into the brick mailbox of their neighbor, Barry Hansen. A ribbon of steam winnowed its way through the now-ruined grill of the Land Barge.

"Dang it," the brothers Kavillehogg moaned in unison.

"Man, that's like, like the fourth time," Jericho said and turned to look out his side window. It was filled with their neighbor Barry Hansen's face, causing Jericho to shriek like a little girl.

Barry shook his head as if to rid it of the sound.

Jericho held up his index finger and shouted, "I'M GONNA ROLL DOWN MY WINDOW MISTER HANSEN!"

The sheer volume caused Barry to grip the frame of the door, knuckles white, as the window had already, despite Jericho's insistence, been rolled down.

"Good gravy, why do you have to shout all the time?" Barry said.

"I DIDN'T REALIZE I WAS SHOUTING... Sorry Mr. Hansen," Jericho said.

"I'm going to have to put in those black and yellow striped concrete-filled steel posts you see outside of cowardly congressmen's offices," Barry said, watching the ribbon of steam escape the hood.

"I'm gonna put this in reverse now, it probably —" Jericho said as he ground the transmission to powder.

"No, wait!" Barry said as the front end of the Land Barge ripped off and fell to the side of the mound of bricks. Steam now billowed out of the front of the Barge, hissing like a demented snake.

Jericho jumped on the brakes with both feet, straining their bodies against the seat belts and then throwing them backward. All they could see was steam.

"It's like we're flying through a cloud!" Jericho said in wonder.

Barry Hansen leaned into the Land Barge and turned off the engine before Jericho could destroy anything else. He looked to both Kavillehoggs and said, "Boys, for my own safety I'm considering moving to the dark side of the moon."

"You won't have to mow any grass up there Mr. Hansen!" Jericho said helpfully.

After a moment, Barry Hansen blinked.

A BUS RIDE TO THE BAYOU

NATHAN AND JERICHO KAVILLEHOGG sat at the bus stop, staring at a billboard ad for the incomprehensibly expensive Italian sports car dealership downtown. It featured a scantily clad woman lighting a cigar for the manly driver using a burning thousand-dollar bill. They stared at it for a long time. A bus came and left while they stared. A second bus wheezed to a stop and groaned as the doors opened. Nathan breathed out heavily and followed his brother onto the bus. Both hung their heads as they mounted the beast.

The bus driver ground several gears into dust before finding the right one to propel the giant aluminum sausage into traffic. The passengers visibly relaxed after it picked up speed.

Jericho threw himself into the seat with a crash, making everyone jump several inches.

Nathan eased himself into the seat just in front of Jericho. Looking around to see that no one was listening, he nodded to himself, satisfied.

"This could be a humungous break for me," Nathan said cautiously over his shoulder.

"Being this is your first case and all, wouldn't *any* case be a big break, little brother?"

"Gosh Jericho, you don't need to — " Nathan said and Jericho playfully hit him in the bicep, causing Nathan to gulp air and wince.

"I'm joshing you, man!" Jericho barked. All the passengers behind them quietly got up and moved several rows back in the bus.

Holding back tears, Nathan said, "Look, this professor is a grand pooh-bah in the marine research community."

"How do you know that?"

"The world wide web."

"The what?" Jericho said, cocking his head slightly to the side like a dumbfounded collie.

The bus started to slow down and everyone waiting for that stop stood up, collected their things, and moved to the center aisle. Then the bus started to speed up, but just barely. Everyone started back for their seats. The bus started slowing down again as the sign for their stop drew near. Everyone's head sagged a bit as they rose again to the aisle. The driver again eased his foot off the brake and the bus just perceptibly gained speed.

Jericho, with the lithe grace and speed of a gazelle, suddenly appeared behind the bus driver who then appeared to levitate six inches in his seat as Jericho lifted him by the scruff of his neck.

"Stop this thing, or I'm going to send you to Bus Driver's Hell," Jericho said with a growl. The bus lurched to a stop. Though it took a few moments to regain their balance, everyone in the aisle stood a little taller, a little prouder. Jericho kicked the door open with his foot. A truly decrepit woman pulled Jericho down and gave him a peck on the cheek as she shuffled by. Grimacing, Nathan squeezed past. Jericho turned to leave.

The Bus Driver muttered under his breath, "Not so tough —"

Jericho spun, causing the Driver to make a sound, not unlike a dog's squeaky toy. Jericho then grabbed the door opening rod and twisted it into, unbelievably, a pretzel shape which he tossed over his shoulder into the street. Jericho made a tight fist — which sounded like someone twisting wet leather and said, "People who have to ride the bus got it hard enough without clutch jockeys like you pumping the brakes." He pointed his pinky at the Driver who appeared to be shrinking.

"I'm watchin' you, Count Punkula!" Jericho said.

The Driver tried not to wet his pants, and failed.

Satisfied with this, Jericho left the bus.

The brothers strode toward the gate of The Wholly Magnificent Bayou Air Boat Ride.

THE WHOLLY MAGNIFICENT BAYOU AIR BOAT RIDE

FIVE MINUTES LATER, Jericho and the proprietor of Wholly Magnificent Bayou Air Boat Rides, both red-faced, stared at each other. Nathan busied himself looking at his shoes. Jericho's eyes bulged a bit; the proprietors did the same.

"This is getting us nowhere," Jericho said.

"I say the same thing, but in a better way," the proprietor countered.

Nathan scrunched his eyes and said, "Huh?"

The proprietor squinted his eyes and said, "You heard me."

"But you didn't say anything in a better way."

"Oh, but I did."

"What kind of Zen double talk is that!" Jericho

said, clenching his fists now that ambiguity had squirmed itself into the conversation.

Nathan started to pull out a tightly wadded ball of one-dollar bills. Jericho gripped Nathan's wrist and shoved Nathan's fist back into the pocket.

"Jericho, can't we just pay like normal people?" Nathan said, his eyes pleading. This caused the proprietor to unscrunch his eyes and arch an eyebrow at Jericho.

"Brought your girlfriend along I see!" sneered the proprietor.

In a blur of motion, Jericho snatched and jerked the proprietor over his head and started spinning him like the blades of a helicopter. It even made the whoop-whoop-whoop sound. The proprietor shrieked like an unhinged parrot and promptly threw up, causing a protective mist of vomit to enclose the two. Nathan ducked and made himself tiny as possible.

"Uncle!" the proprietor managed, goofy sounding now that vomit had clogged his nose.

Jericho slowed and placed the proprietor on the ground. Both wheedled about, arms outstretched, dizzy from the spinning. The proprietor's legs gave way and he ended up performing an impressive cheerleader splitz.

"This is getting us nowhere!" the proprietor said.

"So you'll take the three percent off the ticket price?" Jericho said.

"Two," the proprietor countered.

Jericho reached out for him.

"Three, three, three is what I meant," the proprietor whispered, looking about in case another customer should hear the discount.

"Deal!"

Jericho grasped the proprietor by the shirt and wrenched him up and onto his feet.

"I knew we could find a, what's that word, ummm, — *compromise!*" Jericho proudly said.

Nathan, un-balled himself and stood up. Befuddled he said, "Compromise? In what way?"

The proprietor ambled off toward the airboat.

Jericho slapped Nathan good-naturedly on the back, causing Nathan to come off the ground several inches. Jericho guffawed and said, "He's still alive, isn't he?!"

AIRBOATING THE BAYOU

THE AIRBOAT GLIDED over the water, twisting back and forth with the myriad snaking turns that bayous have. Jericho was in the front of the boat, yelling and shaking his fists at the alligators that scrambled out of their way and up onto the banks.

The proprietor was in awe of this, as he had never known anyone who *could* be heard over the airplane motor three feet behind him.

Nathan was crouched down, gripping the base of the proprietor's seat, his face bright white, looking like a big marshmallow with eyes.

For whatever reason, Nathan had thought that airboats rode on a cushion of air, like a hovercraft. He was decidedly wrong. They are essentially skiffs with an airplane motor bolted in the rear shoving them along. They are steered not by anything in the water, but with a rudder in the air behind the massive propellor just like on an airplane. The boat, in order to turn, had to tip at a scary angle to turn left or right, essentially skipping along the water, very very fast. Nathan was considering a career in the food service industry as the boat slowed to a stop. The plane engine had been throttled down so they could now speak.

Jericho, however, was still in full-throttle mode as he bellowed, "THAT'S AWESOME! THAT BEATS EVERYTHING! HECK, YOU *EARNED* THE FULL PRICE!" Jericho pointed to the proprietor with both hands. "AWESOME, AWESOME, AWESOME!" His last *awesome* was so loud as to cause the bracket holding the airplane motor to ring with harmonic vibration. When Jericho was done yelling, the proprietor and Nathan opened their eyes.

"I'm glad you're enjoying the ride," the proprietor said and looked down at Nathan. "How 'bout you young man?"

Nathan straightened himself as best he could. His body audibly creaked. His hands, however, didn't want to go with the rest of the body. He cleared his dry throat and managed, "I seem to be having a problem getting my hands to let go of these brackets. It would seem they are the only things in this boat with any sense." Nathan leaned over and bit his thumb, which caused his hand to let go.

"Show those hands who is boss, kid!" the proprietor said.

"That's my bro!" Jericho grinned and elbowed the proprietor. Nathan nibbled on the other hand and then stood up and approached the proprietor.

"So, this is it? I would have thought the bayou to be more, well, sprawling and epic," Nathan said and looked distinctly disappointed.

The proprietor shifted from one foot to the other nervously.

Jericho picked up on this. It caused the tops of Jericho's ears to wiggle.

Nathan, seeing his brother's signature ear twitch said, "Well?"

Jericho shot his arms at the proprietor and bellowed, "This man is lying through his missing teeth!" Jericho's shout caused the birds, alligators, and all mosquitoes to flee the area. The bayou was silent. His nostrils then flared out, first the left, then the right. He inhaled deeply and said, "He also only put deodorant under one arm — he skipped a pit." Jericho pointed to the proprietor like a seventeenth-century witch hunter and really let out the stops and shrieked, "PIT SKIPPER!"

Nathan shook his head to clear it after Jericho's unbelievably loud voice. He cleared his throat and said to the boat captain, "Is this true?"

The proprietor turned away from them, raised his arms, and sniffed his own pits. He turned back to them, his head lowered, and said quietly, "Yes."

"To which?" Nathan said.

The proprietor squinted and said, "Huh?" Jericho quickly strode across the length of the small boat causing the proprietor to raise his hands and paw at his own shirt in a good imitation of a gerbil cleaning itself.

"Yes, to which question, you lying liar!" Jericho squeezed out between clenched teeth.

The proprietor pointed to Nathan and said, "I can't help it if he talks like one of them PBS shows. I can't keep up! Yes, I missed a pit, and I'm sorry about that. If my Momma knew she would rise from the grave and spank my behind. And yes, there is more bayou, but no power on Earth, or from the grave can make me take you there."

"But why not?" Nathan said.

The proprietor inched up to the Kavillehoggs and whispered, "Cause I don't want to join my Momma in Death."

The brothers shivered and said, in unison, "Yeesh!"

THE BEAST OF THE BAYOU

THE PROPRIETOR'S shoulders were actually higher than his ears now as he said, "There's a swamp monster, a Bayou Beast, so big it can eat a boat whole and then disappear."

Jericho jammed his hands on his hips and belted out a laugh so loud it caused the proprietor's cap to fly off and into the spinning propeller of the airboat where it burst into fabric confetti. The proprietor sagged and said, "Ah man, and I was just gettin' that thing to stay on my head while goin' eighty miles an hour."

Nathan glared at Jericho and then said to the proprietor, "I am terribly sorry about the loss of your... *cap*. You said the Beast eats boats and submerges. Would you say it is like, say, oh, Jonah and the Whale?"

"Weird, but yeah, just like that. Good call," the proprietor said, giving Nathan a thumbs up, "Yeah, just like that."

"And who's seen this Beast? Like some kinda beer-swilling thrill seekers?" Jericho sneered.

The proprietor scratched his head and said, "Well I don't know about beer-swilling, but FBI Special Agent Betty Catskill *is a thrill seeker.*"

Jericho whipped his head around and said, "FBI, whoa!"

A BRIEF INTERLUDE

THE LAND BARGE shuddered down the highway in an avocado-green blur, sharply pulling to the right whenever Jericho let go of the wheel to unwrap a new protein bar. Nathan, lying down on the rear seat with his eyes squeezed shut and gripping the upholstery said, "If this Special Agent Betty actually saw something, well, gosh, that puts this in a new and rarified light."

Through the wads of protein bars crammed in his mouth, Jericho mumbled, "Super mega-rarified, I'd say."

A LITTLE VISIT TO THE FEDERAL BUREAU OF INVESTIGATION

THE GUARD at the regional FBI office stood up as the brothers Kavillehogg entered. He said, "I need any guns you fellas might be carrying."

Nathan showed two empty palms.

"I got two!" Jericho yelled as he flexed his biceps, which made a sound as if someone were rubbing two pieces of wet rubber together as he pumped his forearms. The guard, clearly impressed, came closer.

Nathan started massaging his own temples and waited for the show to finish.

"Check this out, guardian!" Jericho said as he started pumping faster, his forearms now whistling through the air. The distressed fabric trying to contain the growing muscle began to split and rip.

Jericho's eyes goggled at his own swelling biceps and yelled, "They want out! They need air!" The cuffs of the shirt split and curled like a banana peel up to the bicep. The cuff then burst with a loud pop.

The guard was feebly trying to reach out and touch the red throbbing muscle with his tiny hands as the office door behind them was kicked open.

In the open doorway stood Special Agent Betty Catskill, hands on hips, head thrown back. She said through bared teeth, "What kind of freak show has rolled onto my turf!"

Jericho didn't miss a beat as he said, "Ma'am, admission to the gun show is five dollars!"

The Betty strode over and said cooly, "Let me see if I have anything in the old money belt," and pulled up her shirt a few inches revealing a perfectly ripped set of abs. She smiled as Jericho's bravado faltered and she said, "Do you have change for a six?"

Jericho's eyes welled with tears and he said, "Those are the most perfect abs I've ever seen, perfect. They ain't veiny or nothin'."

The Betty tried to hide her smile and failed, utterly. She then blew on the shredded tassels of Jericho's demolished sleeves causing them to flutter. She laughed and said, "You make your tailor earn his keep too. What can I do for you boys?"

Jericho cleared his throat, explosively.

Mistaking it for a gunshot, the guard reflexively pulled his firearm. The Betty snatched his revolver with her right hand while driving her left into the guard's gut. The guard made a weak 'oof' sound and collapsed unconscious at their feet.

Nathan blanched and gritted his teeth.

She casually flung the revolver onto the guard's desk across the room and commanded, "Into my cave, gentlemen."

Neither Kavillehogg moved. Jericho stared after her. Nathan gaped, his mouth completely open, at the crumpled guard on the floor.

The Betty rammed her head back into the room and barked, "First gear and pop the clutch!"

The brothers jumped four and a half inches into the air and scurried into The Betty's cave.

Unfortunately, not without Nathan managing to catch the guard's nose with his shoe and cause him to trip through the doorway and onto her office floor.

Not waiting for Nathan to get upright, Special Agent Betty Catskill pounded her fist onto her desk and spouted, "Before you start pointing fingers, it indeed *did* take three full magazines of .40 caliber hollow point ammo in the Postal Meter Affair. Postage stamps are more expensive than drugs. Therefore, drug kingpins are nothing, *nothing* like postage thieves. I'm not discussing it anymore. The book is closed!" She then pantomimed a very elaborate hand-washing ritual that would have made Lady Macbeth swoon.

Nathan stood, brushed his pants, and said, "I'm glad *that's* settled."

Jericho's forehead furrowed as if a huge plow had run across it and he went just perceptibly cross-eyed.

Nathan motioned at a chair and said warmly, "May I sit?"

The Betty nodded, and, satisfied at how well things were going punched the intercom button.

Nathan noticed that the intercom's original switch had been crudely replaced with a heavy steel lever and duct taped onto the box, and the tape had been wrapped around it many times.

She barked into it, "Dad, bring us some coffee — *strong*. I want it the consistency of used motor oil... *Dad*?"

Nathan and Jericho exchanged a quick glance.

The Betty gripped the edge of her desk and squeezed the wood, crushing it an eighth of an inch. Two minutes passed as she continued to squeeze the now splintering wood. The guard slowly hobbled in with what was to Nathan the darkest coffee he had ever seen. The glass pot appeared to be spray-painted jet black. When the guard stumbled against her desk and plopped the tray down the coffee didn't slosh in the pot; it didn't move at all. The guard then shuffled out of the room and mumbled over his shoulder, "Remember what the dentist said about that stuff peeling the enamel off your teeth, honey." He slowly shut the door as he left, wheezing.

Jericho jerked a thumb at the door and said, "The guard is your Dad?"

"Uh-huh," she replied as she tipped the coffee pot over the first mug. A pitch-black sludge inched its way down from the pot into the cup beneath it. Nathan held his breath and counted. It took a full seven seconds for the lava-like tentacle to reach the cup. The cup made a crackling sound as it expanded and contracted due to the extreme heat. This caused the cup to slowly creep toward the edge of the desk.

"Yeesh," muttered the brothers in tandem.

"I like my coffee like acid, but thick and hot too!" laughed The Betty, greatly amused. "What can I do for you boys? Ya look kinda — *panicked*."

Nathan was transfixed as the cup inch-wormed its way toward him, fear building in him as he imagined skin graphs and tubs of burn cream in his immediate future.

The Betty pulled on a large silvered fireman's glove and captured the mug before it reached him. She brought it to her lips, causing the brothers to leap to their feet, arms outstretched. She looked them in the eye, winked, and bit off a lump of coffee. They watched in fascination as it stretched out her throat as it went down.

"You're the most amazing woman I've ever met," Jericho said.

"It's true — but obvious," The Betty replied as she blew out a smoke ring.

Nathan couldn't help but think, *That's smoking stomach acid. We must have her as an ally.*

He blurted out, "We need your confirmation of a sighting of a large aquatic reptile, though admittedly, it might possibly be a mammal."

"You want wildlife and fisheries, sugar. I shoot at criminals and break things with my bare hands," The Betty said, turned, and tossed the coffee mug into the air. She drew her gun and blasted the poor cup to pieces slightly smaller than smithereens. Scalding coffee toffee nuggets rained down on the desktop and proceeded to eat holes in it. The guard stumbled in, his gun drawn. The Betty turned to him and started blasting away, shooting him square in the chest, throwing him backward through the doorway. The Betty's giant handgun spun on her trigger finger and was then deftly holstered. Her taut and muscular eyebrows went up, she grabbed a pencil and said, "What can I do for you boys?"

THE BETTY TELLS OF HER BAYOU ADVENTURE

NATHAN BLINKED several times and said, "You just shot your father."

"Yeah," she said.

Nathan blinked several more times and said, "You just shot your father."

She waved her hand at the doorway. "Don't worry, he's wearing his Kevlar vest. Oh God, it's not Wednesday, is it?"

"It's Tuesday. Is that bad?" Nathan said, gripping the armrests of his chair, trying to imagine how it could get any worse.

"Whew, on Wednesday he has his bulletproof vest cleaned. You had me going there for a minute! See, Dad gets trigger-happy, and well, I have to put him down before anyone gets hurt. He'll probably take a nap there on the floor. He's been married to Mom for thirty-one years," The Betty said nodding. "It's hard to scare him — moms are tough!"

The Kavillehoggs, unknowingly, nodded in unison and then said together, "Yes they are." Both seemed to drift a bit.

The Betty snapped her fingers loudly at the boys, and barked, "Stay with me!"

Nathan recovered first. Leaning forward he said conspiratorially, "What we need is any information you can give us on the Bayou Beast."

Before Nathan had finished, The Betty, wide-eyed with fear had her sidearm out and had almost squeezed off a shot into the ceiling, thought better of it, and shoved the gun back in its holster.

She leaned forward and answered him quietly, "I've only been frightened twice. Once, when I plummeted off a sheer cliff with a gasoline tanker truck into a blazing forest fire below. The second, was when I encountered the Bayou Beast. Sugar lumps, I'll take the fiery inferno any day of the week, trust you me! I pack an extra set of underpants now, that darned Beast. What you need there is a tactical nuclear warhead. A small one will do."

Jericho, now enchanted that The Betty had shown a softer side to herself said, "Let's ease into this story. Tell me, uh, us, about the gasoline tanker truck plunging off the cliff into the forest fire. That sounds cool."

This had the intended effect and The Betty shot her massive ripped calves onto her desk, causing an indention in the wood. The Betty's desktop looked like the surface of the moon — cratered and grey.

She said, "It's like this, I was on the trail of some smugglers and I had stolen, uh — *commandeered* a gasoline tanker truck — so that I wouldn't run out of gas during the chase. The bad guys had a hybrid and as you know they can go for a *week* without having to stop. So anyway, we'd been going about forty-seven hours straight now, and wouldn't you know it, we were in the mountains. "

"Which mountains?" said Nathan.

The Betty scrunched her face a bit, "What difference does it make? *Mountains. Big ones!* And now there is this HUGE forest fire at the base of it and I was starting to get tired and hungry." She pointed to Jericho and said, "You know what I mean, it's like I eat six meals a day and it's going on two days now so that's twelve meals now, gone forever, and I started to get a bit *trigger-happy*, if you know what I mean. So anyway, I'm shooting at everything, rocks, the side of the mountain, *clouds*

— you name it. I finally get my act together and shoot the tires off the hybrid and the thing goes silently off the cliff — electric motor, you know. And, well, I was really mad by this time 'cause most cars make a really satisfying VAROOOM sound 'cause the tires are airborne and the motor redlines — but you're detectives, you know this, you've heard it plenty enough. I'm so protein daffy brain tired that I decide to drive the gasoline tanker truck off the mountain and follow them down and put another couple of magazines of bullets in the hybrid just to show 'em. You know, how *mad* I was. In hindsight, yes, it was a *poor plan*. I acknowledge that now. I'm no hothead."

"Clearly," Jericho said, smiling and nodding quickly. Nathan looked at Jericho with trepidation and thought — please don't fall for this woman, we need her, and you, thinking clearly.

Luckily, The Betty was clueless about Jericho's googly eyes and continued with her story.

She said, "The hybrid has like, no air drag at all and shot straight as an arrow into the ground and just crumpled, like a soda can." She then clapped her hands so hard that a subsonic boom was created, shattering the remaining coffee mug on the desk. The coffee slowly oozed out, creating a small fire on the desktop. She rolled her well-muscled left calf across the flames, smothering them.

The brothers, now in mild shock, simply accepted what they saw.

She brushed her calves together. Pieces of smoldering crockery fell to the desktop.

She said, "So my tanker truck is *not* as aerodynamic and tumbled end over end and just burst like an aluminum balloon when it hit the base of the mountain. Gas was just everywhere. *Ruined* my uniform. So I saunter over to the crumpled hybrid and read the smugglers their rights and flex my abs at 'em. They were all pointing at the forest fire and yelling about the gas and going blah, blah, blah."

She shrugged her shoulders as if to say, *people — what can you do?*

Then said, "So I punched into the roof and peeled it back."

"You did what!?" Nathan squeaked.

"I peeled it back, you know, like a sardine can. Stay with me. So I peel the roof off the hybrid and snatch both bad guys by the scruffs of their criminal necks. I shake them real good — it gets the fight out of 'em. Then I look about and realize that our situation had changed, what with the fire coming at us and everything being soaked clear through with gas, but —" The Betty uncurled a single finger, "I'm one of them, *optimists*. Using my bare hands, I dug a shallow grave. I pointed my gun at them and told them to climb into the grave."

Nathan's lips pulled away from his teeth. He then unknowingly pulled an armrest off his chair.

The googliness left Jericho's eyes as he muttered, "High tailin' Jiminy."

She shrugged and said, "They never listen. So I slugged both — with the same punch, by the way — and tossed them into the shallow grave. Then I laid down next to them and pulled the roof of the hybrid over us."

Nathan looked at her for a long moment and his eyes softened. He whispered, "You created a firebreak, then a shelter out of debris, and saved all of your lives. That was genius."

"Yeah, well — *I'm The Betty*."

No one said anything for about thirty-seconds. Then, Nathan leaned forward, as if he were about to ask about a mythical animal, which, in fact, he was. He said, "We can, perhaps, hear more about these postal thieves later. What we really want to learn about is the Bayou Beast. More importantly, what do you think it is? An elephant, or perhaps an abnormally large hippopotamus — ”

The Betty leapt up and twirled her hands about like a helicopter, creating a strong downdraft as her arms cut through the air. “NO! We won’t begin like that!” she yelled at the ceiling and continued, “It is called the Bayou Beast because it is a BAYOU BEAST! I know what a hippo looks like. A hippo! No, no this thing was huge, like convenience store huge, like a double-wide trailer — the kind with the gazebo in the front. Fancy you know, like the Kennedys have, I bet. On the Kennedy compound...” Her revelry about the Kennedys ran its course and she slumped back onto her chair, eyes glazing over, saying to herself, “That Jon-Jon was a good-lookin’ man. Yes he was... ”

“Special Agent Catskill, I would like to —” Nathan began.

“Call me The Betty, sugar, everyone does,” The Betty said.

“The um, *Betty*, how would you physically describe the Bayou Beast? I am trying to find it and someone who has disappeared looking for it.”

“They’ve been eaten.”

Nathan shot forward in his chair, “What?!”

"Honeybun, if you got within a hundred yards of that thing you have become its lunch. He was eaten."

Jericho frowned and said, "What makes you say the person was a man?"

"Women are smart and don't go looking for trouble. No sense lookin' for it, trouble finds you. Every time. I saw the Beast once. That was on another case and I will not return to the bayou unless I fall out of a helicopter during a struggle to wrest the controls from a mad dog killer," she said.

Jericho showed his open palms as if she were stating the obvious and said, "Well, for sure."

"Listen up boys, I was tracking a kidnapper and the trail was hot, red blinkin' hot and I was pushed out of an *airplane* by an accomplice to the kidnappers. I fell through the cypress trees and my fall was broken by two clueless alligators sunning themselves in the wrong place at the wrong time. Hope they're handbags now — they tore my uniform all to blazes," she said.

She shrugged and popped a smoldering coffee nugget into her mouth and blew out another smoke ring. All three watched as the perfect ring drifted away and grew larger and then dissipated into nothing.

She slapped the table hard as she could,

causing the table leg to make an indention on the floor as she shouted to the area where the smoke ring disappeared, "You're distracting me! I'm telling these men what is what! Anyway, it was nearly dusk and the light was terrible. Suddenly, there was a grinding, screeching sound as the cypress trees were shoved to the ground and this AWFUL LARGE BAYOU BEAST WAS THERE AND DESTROYING EVERYTHING IN ITS PATH!"

She snapped her eyes shut and started pounding her thigh repeatedly with her fist, thinning the fabric there. She said, "Therapist said I gotta get *control*, gotta be *mindful*. I'd like to see her be mindful with my fist in her mouth! Crazy? I'll show her what crazy is, I'll — " She looked to the brothers and grimaced. "I don't like talk therapy, I like action."

It was at that moment, Jericho fell madly, helplessly in love with The Betty.

Nathan looked expectantly at her. She shrugged and said, "Its head is like a hammerhead shark — long and sideways. The head is on top of a long neck which is tied into the body that's twice as long as the neck. But the parts are big, real big, like those high-priced RVs that retired military guys drive once a year. It was dark, but by using the muzzle flashes from my gun, I could see the eyes way up high on either end of the head."

She paused to flex her shoulders. It gave the impression that two cats were fighting under her shirt.

Nathan pointed to his eyes and said, "Did the eyes glow red?"

The Betty's shoulders stopped their jig as she lunged forward barking, "You makin' fun of me?!"

Nathan scrunched his eyes shut as tight as they would go and he bolted completely upright, waiting for the killing blow. It never came.

The Betty got herself under a semblance of control and said, "It seemed to be covered in moss and was quiet. Super quiet, that's the scary part! The only noise was the trees being knocked down and crushed. Ever been to the zoo and noticed that the bigger the animal, the quieter it is?" She paused and snapped her fingers. It rang out like a champagne cork.

The brothers Kavillehogg leapt high up, dropped back down, and nodded vigorously.

The Betty, well satisfied, continued, "Elephants, giraffes, you know — they are like ninjas."

She leaned back in the battered chair, way back, almost parallel to the floor, and spoke not to the

Kavillehoggs, but to the ceiling, "When I finally kick off and meet our maker face to face you know what I'm going to ask? Why is it that my cat can't navigate a massive dining room table without knockin' everything down and being loud as a garbage truck? And, to top it off, I can make more noise eating a marshmallow than a Beast as large as an office building? Huh big guy? Why is that?" The Betty shook her fist at the bullet-pock-marked ceiling and said, "Huh? Huh? Just you wait..." Her eyes closed and she drifted off to sleep.

Nathan slowly turned to Jericho and made a walking gesture with two fingers across his forearm. They slowly rose, wincing as the chairs creaked, and slowly made their way through the rubble on FBI Special Agent Betty Catskill's floor.

THE BETTY AWOKE several hours later, glanced at her watch, leapt up, grabbed her gym bag, and bounded over her father's sleeping body. She then jumped out the second-story window into the front seat of her Hum-Vee below. She was two minutes late to the powerlifting competition downtown where she placed first in all categories.

THE BROTHERS KAVILLEHOGG
CONSIDER THEIR OPTIONS

NATHAN SLOWLY LOWERED himself onto the couch in his parents' house, wheezing as he did. Jericho was busy doing pushups in the center of the room. Steam was rising from his sweat-soaked shirt as if a fire was burning inside him, which there was. Not even close to being short of breath, he barked to Nathan, "Hey man, The Betty was really into me, you know?"

Nathan managed to turn his head toward Jericho. He did not bother to try to keep up with the up and down motion of his brother's body. He knew Jericho would not stop unless:

A. The house burst into flames. Unfortunately, that would be unlikely.

B. His left arm was to rebel and snap itself off — also unlikely.

C. An abdomen-distending meal, preferably a buffet, was mentioned, even in an offhand way.

"The Taco Shack of the Damned," Nathan whispered.

Jericho's piston-like motion stopped. He shoved down so hard against the floor that his body shot upright and into a standing position. He shouted, "Let's roll, little brother!"

Nathan held up a limp hand to stop his brother from running into a wall. He cleared his throat and said, "First, we have to make a plan. Remember, we have to get the good professor back before the deadline, which is tomorrow."

"But the tacos!"

"They can wait."

"They can't."

"The restaurant doesn't open for an hour."

Jericho slumped and muttered, "Stupid hours. Hospitals stay open all the time, why not buffets?"

Nathan nodded sagely saying, "I know. The injustice of it all."

Jericho then began shadowboxing, his arms whistling through the air. This in turn created a strong breeze which Nathan enjoyed immensely.

"A plan, please. Those tacos aren't going to eat themselves," Jericho said to his reclined brother.

Nathan slowly turned to a side-lying position so that the downward draft would cool his back. Their parent's couch was a big overstuffed black leather number with lots of brass studs. Really comfortable initially, but a great sweat producer just as you got really comfy and sleepy. It was as if the cows were somehow extracting their vengeance one drop of sweat at a time. The damp spot that had formed at the small of his back cooled instantly, giving him a delicious chill. Nathan cleared his throat and said, "Would you mind doing that, " He then made a sad attempt at boxing and continued, "A bit faster?"

Jericho grinned and really laid on the speed as his arms became a blur.

Nathan's hair started wafting as if he were on the prow of a ski boat. He smiled, knowing that he was the only person on Earth enjoying *this* moment under *these* circumstances. He mused on The Betty's comment about being mindful, closed his eyes, and savored the goosebumps on his back from the chill. The moment passed and, with his eyes closed, eased himself into an upright position. Unfortunately, this was directly in the path of Jericho's hurtling left fist. He literally never knew what hit him.

A MINOR INTERLUDE

NATHAN SENSED his body was sloshing left to right and he heard the sound of crunching bones. He slowly opened his left eye and watched Jericho steer the car with his knees. He was unable to open his right eye due to the swelling created by Jericho's amazing left hook.

Jericho had a really large bag of Capt'n Bob's Cheese Puffs in one hand and a squeezy bottle of barbecue sauce in the other. He would shake some cheese puffs into his mouth and dowse them with a generous squirt of the sauce.

Nathan realized that the crunching was so loud because Jericho was not closing his mouth, simply chewing and swallowing. So efficient was his method that surprisingly little fell onto the floor. The sashaying of his body from left to right was due to the damage to the front end of the car from demolishing the mailbox earlier. The motion, however, was very soothing and it put Nathan promptly back to sleep.

THE TACO SHACK OF THE DAMNED

JERICHO TORE into the parking lot like a police car in a '70s cop show taking the corner so fast as to go on two wheels for about forty feet. Its forward momentum was arrested by several coin-operated animal rides in front of the restaurant. As the Land Barge fell back on all four wheels it crushed the wobbly fiberglass elephant ride. A pool of what appeared to be blood and coins started to ooze out across the sidewalk. This later proved to be all of the Land Barge's transmission fluid.

Ariolano, the manager of The Taco Shack, rushed out and was about to start crying until he spotted Jericho behind the wheel. He rushed to him and then jumped back as Jericho kicked the driver's side door off the car. It clattered and skidded about ten feet. Jericho jumped out and, managing to keep his footing in the spreading transmission fluid slick, hugged Ariolano.

"I thought I was going to miss the opening bell!" shouted Jericho.

"Señor Kavillehogg, my best customer by metric volume!" warbled Ariolano. Both men slapped each other on the back.

"Your accountant called me and said I was the sole reason you stayed open this year!"

"It's true Señor, to my family in El Saltillo, I send panoramic pictures of your feasts. Photoshopped, they say!" Ariolano said, shaking his head. "I myself sometimes believe I am in a dream."

"Is Carla waiting on me today?!" Jericho said, almost clapping.

"Sadly, no, her back is still out from your last visit," Ariolano then brightened, saying, "The bones will heal. She is young and sturdy. But enough chatter — you must eat!"

They strode into The Taco Shack like manly men.

A GOOD FIVE MINUTES PASSED. A burly busboy tromped out and warily prodded Nathan with a small stick. He did not wake. The busboy threw Nathan over his shoulder in a fireman's carry and lugged him toward the restaurant. He then got stuck trying to fit through the door with Nathan draped across him. While rotating in place, the door swung in and conked Nathan a good one in the face as he turned sideways to wedge both their bodies through.

THE TACO SHACK, known to the locals as The Taco Shack of the Damned, had an unusual method of food presentation and service. There were no tables in the Taco Shack. The customers were spread throughout the restaurant on high-backed chairs, some in loose groups, some by themselves. The waitress would take a customer's order and return with their food and drink on a tray attached to their waist and around their neck with a strap just like a hot dog vendor at a baseball game. The customer's food is cut and fork fed to them by the waitress as if her customer was a 150-pound infant. A squiggly 'crazy straw' extended out several feet toward the customer. The act of sucking their drink over such a distance and through the loops was usually enough to wear them down enough that none ever complained about being fed like a baby. In fact, all found this very comforting. Who wouldn't?

THE NATHAN TOTING busboy stopped by Jericho's chair which was directly in front of the kitchen door. This was done as an act of mercy in order to help whoever was *tasked* with feeding Jericho.

Ariolano rushed over and scraped a heavy chair across the entire dining room floor with a tooth-filling loosening screech of metal. Nathan was then unceremoniously slumped upright onto it. Ariolano then placed a tiny sombrero on the back of Nathan's head. It looked like a red felt and sparkly gold sequined donut. He then laced a tiny Mexican flag between Nathan's unconscious fingers. Standing back he nodded at his work and took a Polaroid photo, fanned it a bit, and tucked it in Nathan's waistband.

Jericho dipped his head in Nathan's direction and smiled broadly.

"That's why I come to you Ariolano. You are an artist," Jericho said and slapped his thigh. Ariolano blushed and made a sweeping gesture to the kitchen door.

A large woman slowly staggered out, her serving tray sagging in the middle from the incredible mound of food on it. She wheezed a bit as she stopped in front of Jericho. She then made a beep-beep sound like a truck as she backed up and shuffled her feet so that she rotated to face him. Her face beaded with sweat and she managed, "Señor, I *truly* hope you have brought your best appetite."

"Did you bring the little shovel, Conchita?" Jericho said, barely suppressing his excitement.

She produced not one but two small blue sandbox shovels. She spun them like batons.

Jericho could no longer contain himself and actually clapped.

Conchita's serving tray started to creak loudly. She said quickly, "Señor, we *must* begin."

"Don't wait for me!" Jericho said and opened his mouth so wide that two patrons across the restaurant exchanged a look. One told the other that she thought he had dislocated his jaw like a snake. He had in fact, done so.

Relieved, Conchita ran the shovel around the

perimeter of her tray scooping up an impressive amount of Spanish rice. The little plastic shovel bent precariously as she tried to lift the mound of rice to Jericho's mouth. It shimmied from side to side as she whispered, "Here comes the tiny airplane in to land!"

Jericho closed his eyes and muttered from his gaping maw, "I wish it would dive bomb." She tipped the shovel and spread three-quarters of a pound of rice evenly across his gullet. The rice disappeared like a spaceship tipping past the event horizon of a black hole. She lightly scraped the shovel around his cheeks as a mother would her baby. While she did that she used the *other* shovel to scrape up half a pound of chorizo.

Jericho's eyebrows arched, and said, "A little dive bomber...?"

She waved a single finger, shook her head, smiled, and slowly poured the spicy ground sausage into the black nothingness inside his upturned mouth. She then leaned and whispered into his ear, "Mommasita knows best."

He nodded and muttered, "You do, you do..."

She placed both shovels onto her tray/table and, with an effort, pulled out a large caulking gun mounted under the tray. Loaded in it was a *big* sour cream canister. She ratcheted the handle several times and squished a *quart* of sour cream into Jericho's mouth. She then swapped it out for a battery-powered car buffer. She used it to clear his face and hair of rice that had missed the going away party of their little friends. Jericho's eyes closed as he drifted into a light sleep. She wiped her face with a colorful cloth. Making a beeping sound again, she backed into the kitchen door.

WHAP! Jericho was jolted into consciousness as he was smacked across his dangling jaw. His eyes blinked as his jaw was smacked again. A woman's voice was shouting, "Wake up you slob! Wake up!" He grabbed at his jaw and snapped it back into place with an audible pop. He looked at his attacker.

It was their client, Jacqueline Portsmouth, and boy was she mad. Her face was redder than her hair and Jericho could *swear* that her hair was pointing straight out in all directions. She reared her arm back and started to swing at him again.

As a rule, Jericho doesn't think but, rather, reacts. Perhaps Jupiter was in alignment with Mars that day because he acted with restraint and dignity. He simply held his hand upright in front of his body. When her fist hit his upright forearm it was as if a wad of biscuit dough had been hurled against a steel pole — it just stopped and smushed out in a perfect circle. She was staring at her flattened hand when Conchita shoved a chair behind Jaqueline's knees. This caused Jaqueline to fall ungracefully onto it. Conchita's tray was filled with thirty sapodillas and a galvanized steel bucket of honey. She pushed the tray almost into Jaqueline's chin. Conchita cleared her throat and said, "Señorita, would you like to share dessert with my good friend Señor Kavillehogg? I am so pleased you — woke him from his siesta."

Jaqueline got a hold of herself and laid her flattened hand on her lap with dignity and said, "Thank you, *Señora*, for your offer, but I would rather just speak with my — *friend*." Conchita beeped and backed up several steps and turned toward Jericho, though remaining several feet away from him.

Jericho rubbed the red welt on his chin and smiled. Speaking to Conchita he said, "Please feed me until I burst."

Conchita shoveled up five of the little fried pillows of dough and, pulling the scoop back with her free hand catapulted them from several feet away directly into his mouth. She eased forward and placed the crazy straw into the bucket of honey and planted the curly end into his mouth. He began to suck hard. This caused his cheeks to cave in dramatically. His wanton appetite, however, gave him the strength to pull that honey through all those loops. He leaned back and, breathing hard said, "Miss..."

Jaqueline blinked at this and managed to utter, "Portsmouth, Portsmouth! Gods above, what kind of detectives are you?" She shook her head hoping she was dreaming this. At the end of the shake, she noticed Nathan. Slumped, sombreroed, and with a nasty bruise across his face. She said, "Holy moly, what happened to him?!"

Jericho bought some time by allowing Conchita to catapult more sapodillas into his waiting gullet. He straightened his stuffed body as much as he was able and said calmly, "After a ten-block car chase, because of *your case*, our car has been ruined and he was struck in the face with a heavy wooden door by an unknown uh, culprit person. Unfortunately, my jaw had also been dislocated and I had passed out from the pain. This kind, wonderful person is feeding me. I am not — like you apparently — a superhero. I have to eat now and again."

Turning so red as to become crimson, Jaqueline quickly got up, nodded, and left.

Conchita was smiling ear to ear. Jericho reached out and gripped the edge of her tray/table. She beeped and backed up. This slowly pulled Jericho into a standing position. He took out a fifty-dollar bill and placed it in her hand and curled her fingers around it, patting them. She started to protest and Jericho said simply, "Food is life. All this other stuff we do is wasting time until our next meal. Please ask Ariolano to help us get some wheels. We gotta solve this case before that lady shows up again."

He grabbed the high-back chair Nathan was in and started to drag it to the Taco Shack's entrance. He looked about wistfully at the other patrons enjoying their meals and said, "This case is starting to cut into my eating time. We can't have that."

"ONCE MORE INTO JOE'S CUP OF JOE, MY FRIENDS, ONCE MORE"

THE 'WHEELS' that Taco Shack loaned the Kavillehoggs was an eighteen-wheeler truck with a full semi-trailer. It was cruising down the street pretty fast when Jericho wrenched the steering wheel of the huge truck to the left. It caused the semi-trailer hooked behind it to shudder as it skidded sideways. It smushed many decorative bushes and one rather colorful bunch of flowers. Their seeds wafted up into the air and, with luck, would settle and germinate in a place where *no* Kavillehogg has a license to operate *any* motor vehicle.

Jericho wrenched open his door and strode purposefully to the passenger side and tugged on the door handle. It made a hollow clacking sound and remained there smugly unopened, like an obstinate schoolboy. Jericho would not be one-upped by a mechanical device — not now, not ever. He gripped the handle so hard that it was dimpled, then twisted his hand in a tight circle. The metal surrounding it wrinkled and tore away like cheap tissue. He was about to tell the door who indeed was the boss when it swung open by itself. Jericho jumped back, startled.

Nathan slowly clambered down and stretched. He brought his hands down and frowned at the tiny Mexican flag laced in the fingers of his left hand.

"How did you get that door open?" asked Jericho, confused.

"I was dreaming about a terrible ripping sound, woke up and unlocked the door," yawned Nathan.

Jericho put his hands behind his back and tried to pull the mangled handle free as he said, "It was locked? *Huh.* Well, how 'bout a cup of Joe?"

Nathan walked past Jericho and through the doorway.

The surly door handle enjoyed the last laugh as Jericho had to bend over, stand on the mangled metal and wrench his hand upward. The fingers stretched and all the knuckles popped, but the hand came free. Jericho waved the hurt hand and looked about before he muttered, "Ouchy." He then became angry with himself for saying that and punched his leg with his bad hand. He grunted and said, "Ouchy-ouch." He then stood straight and marched into Joe's Cup of Joe as if he not only owned *it*, but the coffee plantations where the beans came from as well.

A PLAN TO END ALL PLANS,
PART ONE

NATHAN WAVED at Jericho from the far end of the bar with a small trowel covered in caulking or something that resembled caulking. Nathan also had what appeared to be a small white toilet bowl in front of him. "I've ordered the Grandeisimo Largeio," he said.

The barista, Joe, found the job title — barista — too cutesy for a grown man and demanded that everyone just call him Joe. Joe reached over and pulled Jericho close so he could whisper, "What on God's green Earth is on your brother's head?" Only then did Jericho notice that Nathan was still wearing the tiny sombrero.

An image floated unimpeded through Jericho's mostly empty brain. It was of Ariolano with a big metal stapler, affixing the sombrero to Nathan's head. Ka-chink, ka-chink, ka-chink.

Jericho smiled and shook his head to empty his mind once more. He said, "It's Mexico Day or something."

Joe waved a little Mexican flag and said, "That would explain this. He handed it to me when he came in. I thought it was Irish, or Indonesian or — *something*. I was busy in high school looking at a girl named Nancy when they were teaching us that stuff. I shoulda been listening."

"That makes two of us. I was always daydreaming about lunch, my friend. I just ate, but the drive has made me a bit peckish," Jericho said boldly.

"The food truck out the window says The Taco Shack. That's just down the street."

Jericho spread his hands far apart and said, "Exactly."

"I hear ya. We have cream-filled donuts," Joe said, then turned and winked at Nathan. He returned his attention to Jericho as he said, "But filled with, get this — a quarter pound of *wedding cake icing*."

Jericho's eyes crossed slightly and he fainted.

Joe looked down at the inert body and then put

his hand out to Nathan, palm up saying, "Pay up buddy, five bucks."

Nathan crinkled his nose and said, "I would have never agreed to this wager if I had known it was wedding cake icing. That is like heroin to a foodie. This is completely unfair."

Joe looked at Nathan with steely eyes and said, "Pay up you welsher, or I'm taking away your little potty that also happens to be filled with *wedding cake icing*."

Nathan put his arm with the little trowel around the tiny commode like a prisoner at mealtime. With his free hand, he pulled out a five, tossed it on the bar top and said, "You're a hard man, Joe."

Joe snatched up the money, sniffed it, and muttered, "Gotta be, with customers like you two. How are we gonna get him up? Anyone got an appliance dolly?" He looked about to his patrons. All had the dazed looked of being in a sugar stupor. He sighed and deftly hopped over the bar top with a sticky bun in his hand. He crouched and wafted it under Jericho's nose. Jericho's head snapped forward and bit down on the sticky bun and almost into one of Joe's fingers.

"Cancel the appliance dolly!" Joe said and thrust his hand down to Jericho, who grabbed it. Joe, with a superhuman amount of effort, heaved Jericho into an upright position. He gripped Jericho's bobbling head with one hand and waved three fingers in front of it saying, "How many?"

Jericho shook his head. There was a barely audible rattle.

"One," Jericho said.

Joe and Nathan exchanged a look.

"One Grandesimo Largeio toilet bowl of *WEDDING CAKE ICING!*" Jericho bellowed so loudly that a cat howled outside.

Though Joe's eyes were watering from the volume, he smiled and leapt back to his side of the bar. He crouched and hefted up a smallish fake toilet bowl and little trowel. He proceeded to fill the bowl with enough icing to give a team of cardiologists the willies. He gripped the base and gave it a hard shove.

It shuddered down the bar into Jericho's waiting paws. He took the trowel and scowled. "Don't you have anything *man-sized?*" Jericho said.

Joe shook his head, wagged a finger, and said, "You gotta slow down, taste, savor, and appreciate what I have created. This isn't something from a grocery store. It's got texture, it's aromatic, it's an — *experience.*"

Jericho looked from Joe to trowel. In his hand, it

really did look tiny. A long moment passed. "Don't you have anything *man-sized?*" Jericho said.

Nathan leaned over and whispered in Jericho's ear.

Jericho's shoulders sagged and he said quietly, "Please?"

Joe folded his arms and then unfolded them. He folded them again. He frumped and said, "I gotta step outside. You wanna get the giant quart-sized scoop, get it yourself." He turned and started to schlep toward the back door.

Jericho bounded over the bar. He was almost to Joe, who whimpered, "Please don't kill me!" Jericho grabbed Joe and lifted him off the ground. Joe yelped like a puppy. Jericho shook Joe and then held him in a bear hug.

"I'd never kill ya, Joe! Who'd make the coffee and donuts?!" Jericho said as he placed Joe on the ground again and continued, "I shovel food because I love it. You want to see me uh, savor something — watch me eat steamed broccoli. It would take me a *week* to eat one of those flavorless tree-shaped things. But this?" He made a flourish with both arms at the pastry case and said, "It's like air, like, it's like *love* made solid, sweet, and edible. I've never actually been in love, but if it's like this?" He grabbed a double-glazed bear claw and dropped it in his open mouth. He didn't chew, it just fell straight into his waiting belly. "If love is like this, I want it, and I want it all. I want big, big portions. *Don't live life with little spoons.* That's just getting along. That's for them!" Jericho said and pointed out the window at the people trudging down the street, their heads down, looking a few feet ahead of them, oblivious of the glorious world all about them.

He picked Joe back up and set him on the bar top.

"I want to know I've been to Joe's Cup of Joe. I want to be *on that mountaintop*, not just watch it on TV," Jericho said and stared at his brother. "Or read about it in a book, little brother. You asked me about self-esteem. I just *do* things. If I want to do something or eat something, or — *whatever* — I *do* it. Our grandfather doesn't sit around and tell us about what he did, does he? He tells us about *what he didn't do, about what he'd wish he'd done.* I can't — I *won't* — be that way." He spun, shot a hand under the counter, and lugged out a really impressive stainless steel scoop.

It was big. Like Texas.

Jericho slapped the steel scoop against his abs, denting the scoop and causing it to ring. He said,

"Now let's eat a fake toilet bowl full of wedding cake icing and solve this mystery!" He nodded to Joe, hopped over the bar top, and dropped onto his barstool.

Nathan was staring at him, his mouth slightly open. Jericho reached out and gently closed it and said, "To keep the flies out."

Joe grinned, snapped his bar rag with a proud pop, and went on to polish the glass pastry case to a brighter shine than it had when it rolled off the factory floor.

A PLAN TO END ALL PLANS,
PART TWO

EIGHT MINUTES later they were about halfway down into their respective potties and agreed to stop and get down to 'brass tacks' whatever *that* meant.

"I'm stymied," Nathan admitted, icing slathered all about his face.

Jericho's eyes dilated as he concentrated hard and said, "Does that mean you're not sure what to do next?"

"Yes."

"Oh good, because I have an idea," Jericho said and put his hands around his hard belly. An ominous sound rumbled down there. "I think even I have eaten too much," Jericho said and then belted out a laugh. He shoved his 'scoop of plenty' deep into the toilet bowl and it came up with a heaping wad of sugary goodness.

Nathan saw his chance and put his hands between the scoop and Jericho's gaping maw. Jericho's lips pulled back in the beginnings of what was going to become a snarl.

"Whoa now, I just wanted to hear the plan before you eat that — *healthy portion*," Nathan said. "We're on something of a time limit you see. Miss Portsmouth has been very patient. We haven't heard from her yet, which is good."

Jericho's lips unsnarled and he said offhandedly, "That's the lady with flaming red hair, right?"

Nathan nodded and said, "In the business, we call her a *client*."

Jericho nodded and tried very hard to concentrate on their conversation *and not* on eating the fluffy, delectable icing that was calling to him like a Greek siren. He said, "I agree. We don't want her mad at us thinking we've not been hard detecting, instead of say — eating."

"I don't think our client would begrudge us a tiny snackipoo like this. To keep our energy up and all. It's not like we've been eating a sit-down meal at a restaurant," Nathan said and laughed at his own joke.

Jericho was very still. The conversation/need for icing strain was coming to a breaking point. This caused his tongue to bypass the uptight, so-called 'reasoning center' of the brain. His tongue slowly extended out to the waiting pile of icing. It touched it and, satisfied it was indeed still there and not some dream dreamed up by the big dumb brain it relaxed and allowed Jericho to breathe again. Oxygenated, the frontal lobe of the brain was allowed to do its thing, which was to keep the rest of the body out of trouble.

Jericho said, "Yeah man, I don't think she would begrudge us a snacky snack. Also, we should get closer to the bayou, like pronto. So she won't as you said, like track us down herself."

Nathan nodded and laughed at this.

Jericho's frontal lobe, satisfied it wasn't going to get in trouble in the next few minutes, gave priority to the right hand to feed away. The great scoop approached the mouth's opening and the tongue extended like an old friend to help it find its way home. The upper brain, not being used most of the time and therefore quite lazy, completely shut down for the next few minutes during *the shoveling*.

Nathan recognized his brother's mental disconnect and ordered a sugary, milky, frothy drink with a smidge of coffee. This was so it could be legally called a 'coffee drink.' He rather enjoyed these moments of quiet, imagining this is what it must be like for other brothers, moments of quiet contemplation and fellowship being mostly —.

CRASH!!!

Jericho's little toilet bowl had fallen to the ground and shattered like a tiny atomic bomb. Jericho's hand/scoop was still making a scooping motion, blindly searching for the source of fun which was, sadly, no more. He had, in his sugar stupor, pushed the bowl over the edge of the bar top as a dog will propel an empty dog food bowl around and around as if by sheer motion, more food would be produced. None was left. The food parade was over. Joe came over with a broom and an almost comically large dustpan. Nathan cringed when he saw what was written in magic marker along the shaft of the dustpan — The Kavillehogg Express.

Joe swept for about five minutes and wheezed as he lifted the enormous dustpan with both hands. It creaked and buckled, but held. Joe waddled away with the load and turned the corner.

Nathan took a fork off the counter and jabbed it into Jericho's thigh. Jericho's left eye blinked and he slowly came back to life.

"Oh hey man, ready to go?" Jericho muttered, the icing around his chin having formed a five-inch stalactite. He looked like a parody of a 1908 black-and-white movie villain. Nathan couldn't suppress a laugh.

"First, we must discuss your plan," Nathan said, grabbed the stalactite, and snapped it off.

"Yeah, uh well, sure," Jericho said, clearly unsure.

Nathan closed his eyes.

"Look brother, I have a plan, but I don't think it is like the plan to end all plans though. It's no Bay of Pigs, you know," Jericho said, nodding.

"The Bay of Pigs invasion was a total disaster," Nathan said.

"Oh. They made a big deal out of it so I thought it was like this whatcha call a masterstroke," Jericho said.

"Well, you're wrong. It was a disaster for the Kennedy administration," Nathan said.

Jericho eyed Nathan's still intact toilet bowl.

Nathan raised the icing stalactite in a defensive motion and mouthed the word NO.

Jericho looked at his hands and said, "Anyway I thought it was the Bush guy's thingamajig."

"No. Anyway, which Bush?" Nathan said,

interested in the first mention of politics from his brother.

"There were two?" Jericho said simply.

"Yes."

"Gosh," Jericho said. "So much to keep up with..."

Nathan fought the compulsion to stab Jericho. Instead, he closed his eyes and thought of the rows of beautiful books in the Bodleian Library at the University of Oxford in England. The stabbing compulsion passed. He put the stalactite down and pried the scoop from Jericho's fingers. Nathan was impressed. The scoop looked as if it had been polished. He nodded his appreciation of the skill and then held down Jericho's hands onto the bar top to prevent them from foraging for food.

"Tell me your plan. Now. I don't care what you think of it. I believe in you, and perhaps we can together come up with what, as you say, is the plan to end all plans," Nathan said, while inside his brain all the logic centers shook their collective heads at this folly.

Jericho, emboldened, sat at his full height and began, "We get to the bayou, get a boat and —"

Nathan bolted upright as if he had sat on an unusually large tack whimpering, "Not the airboat..."

Jericho retrieved his mighty scoop and gently touched Nathan's drooping shoulder with it and said, "Yes, the airboat. You have said like three hundred and nine times that we are out of time. The professor/doctor/whatchahaveit has to be wherever at nineish for this conference or the world will stop spinning or whatever, right?"

Nathan nodded.

"Okay, so we get on the airboat and go all over the bayou until we meet up with this Bayou Beast thing and take care of it. If it has eaten the professor guy whole and this thing is as big as The Betty says it is, he should still be alive inside of it," Jericho said and put down the scoop of plenty.

Joe limped back in, massaging his lower back with his free hand. Jericho motioned for him to come over. Joe paused. Jericho belted out a laugh and then said for all to hear, "We're done. For now. Check please!"

"But we haven't discussed this yet!" Nathan said.

"Oh yes we have, little brother. When I said it out loud just now, I kinda found that *it is* the plan to end all plans. I like it!" Jericho said and squared his shoulders, air whooshing past as he did.

"But we haven't discussed it. We need a *dialogue*," Nathan squeaked.

"Oh. Got anything to add?" Jericho said.

A long moment passed.

Jericho grew bored and flexed one pec muscle and then the other, faster and faster to the beat of a tune playing in his head.

"Well, um, I suppose I do not have anything to add. It just seems so — *simple,*" Nathan said.

Jericho tossed some cash on the bar top and said, "Simple plan for simple people. Let's roll!"

A QUICK TRIP TO THE ARMY/NAVY SURPLUS STORE

NATHAN LOOKED about the cabin of the Taco Shack truck. He returned again and again to the colorful, large Chihuahua flag, rubbing the silky fabric between his fingers. He thought for the five hundred and seventeenth time that he wished the United States flag was as simple and bold looking as that. What if we add another State? Is that Star going to be on the bottom row all by itself? It would lose all symmetry! He knew he had to change his thought pattern before he pulled out a sketch pad and began mailing new flag concepts and cloth swatches to his congressmen and senators. *Like the last time.* He shuddered.

"Jog my memory. How did we end up with the Shack's eighteen-wheeler as our mode of transport?

The last vehicle I remember being in was Dad's Land Barge," He said, clearly confused. He went to scratch his head and came back with a tiny sombrero. He frowned, but not unhappily. He rather liked sombreros, and this one was purple, his favorite color.

Jericho could not remove his eyes from the dinky purple hat. He cleared his throat and said, "Well — it's a boring story."

Nathan felt under his seat and pulled a frighteningly large, rusty machete out of its scabbard that was affixed there. He started to play with it, making 'swoosh-swoosh' noises. He turned the razor-sharp edge up and dropped the diminutive hat over it. The hat was effortlessly sliced in two as it drifted down upon the blade. Nathan frowned at this and very carefully put the big, big, big knife back where it belonged. He turned to Jericho and said, "Then bore me."

Jericho double-clutched, the truck shuddered and he said, "I damaged the Land Barge while — parking it. Ariolano was very cool and let us borrow his wheels."

"But there are eighteen of them!"

"You little brother, are a snob."

"I'm a realist. Where do we park this thing?!"

Nathan said, hitting his fists against his thighs. He continued, "Could you think of anything *less* maneuverable? It's like a strip mall on wheels!"

Jericho had stopped listening, however. He had spotted an opened bag of ranch dressing & ghost chili-flavored nuts on the floor of the truck's cabin. It was almost empty, just a few stragglers left. Pinching his shoes together, he lifted them up, looking like a giant ballerina that could defy gravity by sheer willpower alone. He brought the sad little bag to his grasping hand. The few remaining nuts were deftly delivered to his waiting mouth. They were then dispatched to digestive oblivion. He said, through a tendril of smoke caused by the ghost chili half of the nuts, "You're obviously upset. I'm gonna throw back at you what you've been feeding to me for years — this conversation no longer serves a purpose." He smirked, saying, "Now watch as I power brake this baby. One hundred and eighty degrees!" He jumped on the brakes and jerked the wheel hard to the right.

The trailer of the truck shuddered and swung one hundred and eighty-five degrees, essentially turning the truck around in the opposite direction, tires chittering and smoking, narrowly missing several cars. It slammed to a stop against the curb. The massive trailer teetered and looked as if it was going to fall over onto several pedestrians. All but one lady ran. She instead shot her arm out and pointed at the swaying truck as if she were in a Japanese monster movie. The truck, with the help of its friend, gravity, tottered upright.

She was still pointing, her mouth agape as Jericho leapt down from the truck, landing next to her. Using his pinky, he gently moved her chin up, closing her mouth. He said to her, "Pretty sweet job of parking this baby, huh?! I'm a professional."

"A professional what?!" she said.

Jericho leaned close and, looking about as if revealing nuclear codes said, "Food taster, ma'am. You know, for the snack food industry. I'm just helping out my little brother here to solve a mystery. I'm the brains you see. Don't tell him — he's sensitive. The factory I taste for is chugging away 24/7 replenishing the food I eat, uh, test. They need to be more clear as to how much they want 'tested'. You know how it is. Take it easy now!" He snapped his heels and marched into One-Armed Bob's Surplus Store.

She was staring after Jericho as Nathan clambered down the side of the truck cabin. She stopped Nathan and said, "Is that maniac a food tester?"

Nathan tiredly said, "And more madame, and more." He pulled out a black 'unbreakable' comb and straighten the part in her hair and lowered her arm. He shuffled off to the store.

The woman looked at what Nathan had done with her hair in her reflection on the side of the truck. She liked what she saw, smiled, and strode down the sidewalk, a little pep in her step.

ONE-ARMED BOB'S SURPLUS STORE

LIKE ALMOST ALL military surplus stores, it was a strange mixture of Belgian army World War One actual surplus with the remainder being new items made in China. Items such as 'camo' fatigue pants with an incomprehensible number of pockets.

Jericho was gaping at the *fightin' knives* case. There were well over 100 styles of mauling and Bowie-style knives. Double, triple-edged with 'blood gutters' and 'gut hooks.' It would have given Torquemada hives. Jericho's breathing was shallow and rapid.

Nathan tapped Jericho's shoulder. Jericho didn't notice. He tried again without result. He tried a different tack and whispered, "All-you-can-eat snack cakes."

Jericho spun, fire in his dilated eyes, his lips sputtering, "WHERE?!" He got a hold of himself and tried to slow his breathing. He was unsuccessful. Between breaths, he said, "You should know better, little brother. People have *strokes* because of that sorta thing!"

Nathan was abashed — but just a little, saying, "Listen, what are we here for? We aren't going in the military."

Jericho leaned close and said, "Weapons of minor destruction. We are going to kill the Bayou Beast."

Nathan cringed inwardly and looked about. With the exception of the *fightin' knives* case, there didn't seem to be anything remotely dangerous; the camo thongs being, perhaps, an isolated example.

"You use these knives to carve out the hearts as a trophy of the kill. The real weapons are in the secret armory around the back. We gotta find One-Armed Bob," Jericho said and nodded to the rear of the store by the hammocks and little folding shovels. He cupped his hands to his mouth. Nathan quickly jammed his fingers in his ears as Jericho bellowed, "BOB!!!" The front window glass shimmered and produced a fine latticework of hairline cracks.

A wrenching mechanical sound, not unlike a

junkyard compactor crushing a Soviet tank's transmission came echoing throughout the store. Nathan blanched and whimpered, "You've damaged the foundation of the building. It's going to collapse and bury us alive."

Jericho smiled and said, "Nah man, that's One-Armed Bob. He's what people in the 1970s TV shows called a *cyborg*."

Nathan's head appeared to be retracting into his body, like a big pale turtle. He said, "Like a robot with a human head!?"

A deep voice behind Nathan said, *"No kid."*

Nathan was so frozen by fear that his neck wouldn't turn to look at the voice. His eyes, however, didn't have the good sense to close. They saw metal fingers clamp down on his left shoulder. He only *thought* that he blanched earlier. He was so pale now that his skin blended with his white undershirt. The fingers gripped his shoulder more tightly.

The rumbling voice said, *"Just the arm."*

Nathan's eyes threw in the towel and rolled up into his head as he passed out. He did not fall, however. The mechanical arm held Nathan upright, in a parody of a standing position. The hand tipped Nathan a bit and Nathan's body jiggled as if he was a marionette.

Jericho couldn't help but laugh. He looked past the mechanical hand and said, "One-Armed Bob, you are a hard man."

One-Armed Bob gave a deep rumbling laugh and said, "You gotta be, kid. Ya gotta be! What can I do for you, my royal food taster?"

"You got anything that can kill say, a medium-sized dinosaur?"

"I have just the thing! Though it may be more in line for a large one though," One-Armed Bob said and laughed again as he trudged toward a hidden door, tipping Nathan from side to side making it seem as if he were doing an Irish jig.

IN THE SECRET ARMORY

ONE-ARMED BOB STOPPED at the black metal door. He leaned forward and placed his eye against a retinal scanner. It beeped and the door slowly opened. Beyond it was an h-u-g-e room lit by red lamps. There were swords. There were guns. Mortars. Bazookas. Whips. Pen knives. Lawyers briefcases. Anything that could inflict pain was there — and more! One-Armed Bob's eyes welled with tears and said, his voice horse, "It's just so *beautiful.*"

Like everyone, One-Armed Bob had issues, it is true. *Inflicting hurt* was not one of them.

He rotated and set Nathan down on the chair of an anti-aircraft gun. He turned to Jericho and said, "What's it going to be? M-16, rocket-propelled grenade, the old standby — a heat-seeking missile?"

"No, like I said, this thing is huge, like several rent-to-own stores stacked three high — really!" Jericho said and shrugged.

"So it's an Indian elephant you're hunting!" One-Armed Bob said and swept his arm to a Mini-Gun by his side.

The name Mini-Gun is terribly misleading; there is nothing *mini* about it. It is, in fact, a six-barrel electric rotating Gatling gun. It requires thousands upon thousands of rounds of ammo which are enclosed in a backpack along with the batteries for the gun's motor. It was originally designed to be bolted to the fuselage of a helicopter in order to *cut enemy aircraft in two* with its insane thousands of rounds per minute rate of firepower.

"Hey man, that looks cool!" Jericho said and automatically started to reach out to fondle the gun. One-Armed Bob clacked his fearsome hand several times like a lobster's claw up in Jericho's face to stop him from touching the Mini-Gun. Jericho laughed and said, "Sorry man, it's just too tempting!"

"Don't I know it!" One-Armed Bob chortled, and continued, "Just what are you two going to send back to its maker?"

Jericho glanced at his brother's sleeping form

and said, "Well, it will probably be just me — my brother here doesn't like the idea of killing anything."

One-Armed Bob smirked and said, "Like that bacon he had for breakfast? Did the pig get depressed and commit suicide?"

"Yeah, I know. What's the word for that?" Jericho said.

"When you're against something, but do the same thing in a different way? It's uh —" One-Armed Bob said and tapped his oversized iron hand against his teeth, clinking away as both pondered.

A good three minutes passed as they thought, shifting their weight from one foot to the other.

"Times up!" One-Armed Bob proclaimed, proudly.

Jericho waved at Nathan and said, "Maybe we should wake him up. He would know the word you know — ka-zing — just like that! He reads a *lot*."

"*Huh*. Big books?" One-Armed Bob said and looked warily at Nathan.

"Like you wouldn't believe. He says he likes big books, and he cannot lie!" Jericho managed to say while laughing.

One-Armed Bob's head tilted to one side like a confused poodle. He said, "I did a lot of drugs in the

60's — it doesn't matter. Anyway, what are you guys hunting? Please be precise."

Jericho avoided the other man's eyes and said under his breath, "A Bayou Beast."

The metal fingers started clacking together like a crab having drunk an entire pot of espresso. One-Armed Bob danced a little jig.

"You believe in the Bayou Beast?" Jericho managed.

"Believe? BELIEVE?! Come with me — now!" One-Armed Bob said as he made a beeline to the back of the secret armory.

Jericho had to almost run to keep pace. He suddenly stopped to gawk at a big machine gun bristling with a grenade launcher, underslung shotgun, and multiple laser thingies. Jericho was acting like a wind-up toy, his mouth moving silently, his head nodding in agreement with his throbbing ego — which was poking his brain with a sharp stick.

Jericho was broken from his revelry by two iron fingers pinching and then twisting his earlobe. "Ouchy ouch!" he said before he could catch himself.

One-Armed Bob said, "Sorry kid, I didn't mean to getcha so hard. That measly gun won't scratch the Bayou Beast!"

"Really?" Jericho was flummoxed. He looked at the gun again. It seemed able to destroy anything — and without breaking a sweat doing so.

"That magnificent weapon would achieve one thing," One-Armed Bob said, soberly.

"Which is?" Jericho murmured.

"It would make it angry. Well, *upset it,* at any rate," One-Armed Bob said, clearly peeved that any of his weapons could manage anything less than sending its intended target into the afterlife, pronto. He turned to a shiny chromed orb jutting from the wall. He gripped it with his Iron Fist of Oblivion. Sparks flew and One-Armed Bob's body was enveloped in a bizarre blue glow. His hair — what there was left of it — stood up as if hearing the national anthem. A secondary panel, heavy and thick, slid to the slide with a wretched scraping sound. A noise that was as if someone took a rusty flat-end shovel and drug it across some humongous chalkboard. He released the orb. His body glowed for a moment more and returned to normal.

"Wow, you look, well, younger," Jericho said, clearly impressed.

"Yeah, that was 92,000 volts. Jazzes you up a bit. It's cleared my complexion up too!" One-Armed Bob said, playfully showing both sides of his face and smiled.

"But, but, how did you survive that?!" Jericho said, backing away slightly.

"Go easy, it's a con man's trick. When I grab the ball thingy it grounds me and the electricity passes through me, kapisch? Lots of volts won't hurt you. Lots of amps, however, will. Like, kill you," One-Armed Bob shrugged. "Looks cool though, doesn't it?" He quickly grabbed Jericho's wrist with his amazing iron hand, dragged him to the orb, and said, "Check this out!" He slammed Jericho's hand onto the orb and held it tight. The hair on both their heads saluted the flag and they glowed and sparked in unison.

"THIS IS AMAZING! LIKE BEING ON AN AIRBOAT BUT WITH 92,000 VOLTS COURSING THROUGH YOU! WE NEED MORE!!!" Jericho bellowed and suddenly spied the nearby wall socket.

One-Armed Bob quickly added one and one together and yelled, "You can't, that plug isn't grounded, we will be —"

Jericho's upper 'reasoning brain' had by this time, however, been hijacked by the lower 'rascal brain'.

He jammed his pinky in the wall socket. 92,110 ungrounded volts were unleashed and a thunderclap was created.

The two adventurers were blown through the open doorway into the *Secret, Secret Armory*. Jericho was thrown fifteen feet and struck a metal cabinet stenciled Fragile/Motion Sensitive Landmines/Do Not Vibrate. He struck it headfirst and so hard that his face made a three-and-a-half-inch clean indentation in the thick metal. All he would have to do is pour plaster into it and he would have an attractive mask suitable for display.

One-Armed Bob fared a little better in that he had launched up and at a slight angle and was now hanging from a ceiling fan, spinning in a slow lazy circle. He had the appearance of a superhero with a very limited flight radius.

"Hey man, you cool?" Jericho said very slowly, his already overtaxed little brain still trying to cope with the extra burden of 92,110 volts racing through the few neural pathways there.

One-Armed Bob was a stoic and attempted a shrug of his shoulders during rotation. He said, "Fine kid, fine. There is a manual release for my *Iron Fist of Death*, let me just find it here before I become too dizzy." He fidgeted with several knobs and levers on his metal forearm with little success. He brought his fleshy hand to his chin and pondered his place in the cosmos for a moment. This philosophical break was short-lived, however.

A sound like someone dumping an infinite number of horseshoes into a finite number of in-sink garbage disposals hit his ears. That sound ended, only to be replaced by several minutes of thousands of bullet ricochets ping-ping-pinging and then blessed silence.

One-Armed Bob broke the silence saying, "It would appear neither Kavillehogg brother can resist messing with the Mini-Gun."

Below the rotating stoic, Jericho put his hands on his hips, nodded, and said, "It's like a big red button that says don't touch!"

One-Armed Bob reflected on this and responded, "Hmm, I suppose it does. Would you mind checking on him? Oh, and turning off the fan switch? It's right next to the three-ton sliding panel."

"Sure, but you want me to help you down?" Jericho said, his arm extended and circling to keep pace with One-Armed Bob.

"No, please go ahead. I'm going to consider

another, perhaps safer career. Like, say, bomb disposal. Go on, he's that way," One-Armed Bob said and motioned with his free hand to find Nathan, made all the more confusing by his rotation — it seemed to direct Jericho to all four corners of the secret, secret armory.

"Okay man, but I'm going to try the other room first," Jericho said and stumbled out of the room on his still rubbery legs.

One-Armed Bob continued to turn and turn, Jericho having forgotten to flip the switch on his way out. He breathed out slowly and said, "Well, it is, possibly, safer up here anyway."

———

JERICHO GLANCED about the first secret armory. The lights were flickering and there appeared to be nothing left unscathed. Every single object in the room had either a smoking bullet hole or a ricochet dimple.

Nathan's head slowly rose out of the dust and smoke, both eyes squeezed tightly shut. With the help of his fingers, he managed to open one, and seeing the carnage, the other opened by itself —

albeit with reservations. Both of his pupils dilated at the wreckage and he mumbled, "Golly."

Jericho couldn't help but laugh and said, "Man oh man, little brother. Your first case is racking up the expenses quick."

Nathan looked to Jericho and then squinted. He closed his eye and then looked again and said, "What on Earth has happened to your hair? You look like the synthesizer player for an 80's glam rock band."

Jericho was making a fist and drawing back his arm when he noticed his hair in a shattered mirror. His first impression was that a helmet had dropped on his head. A sober closer look revealed that his once long hair was now in a big tight perm, curled by the high voltage. He let out an involuntary chirp, like a demented sparrow.

Nathan touched it and said, "But the ladies are going to fight over you."

Jericho relaxed his fist and touched the spongy, tight curls. He wistfully said, "That's true. I only hope it doesn't need a lot of product."

Nathan patted Jericho's tight 'fro once more and let him lead the way into the secret, secret armory. His gaze was immediately drawn to the rotating figure above. He looked about and flipped the switch.

The fans quickly slowed. One-Armed Bob was trying several more tiny levers on his metal forearm when he suddenly dropped like a wet sack of chicken thighs toward the table of bear traps that had been waiting patiently for him.

IN THE SECRET, SECRET ARMORY

NATHAN'S upper brain freaked and his eyes slammed shut.

Jericho's entire brain had given up and turned on the 'closed' sign.

But one doesn't live to be to One-Armed Bob's age without being cunning and wily. He had a plan. His body tumbled midair like an Olympic high diver so that he was now plummeting headfirst toward the gaping maws of the bear traps. He shot out his *Iron Fist of the Apocalypse.* There was a single SNAP and CLANG.

"Whoa!" Jericho said.

Nathan overrode his brain and unsqueezed one eye. He saw One-Armed Bob doing a single-arm handstand, the iron fist caught in the powerful jaws of a really large trap. One-Armed Bob winked at Nathan and 'hopped' onto the next bear trap with a CLANG and then another. He had collected four by the time he reached the edge of the table. With his iron arm totally encrusted in grisly-looking traps he did a back flip off the table and landed sure-footedly in the center of the aisle. He shook his arm once and the traps flew off and onto the floor where they snapped at each other like giant wind-up joke teeth. They stopped and the silence was complete.

The brothers clapped politely as if One-Armed Bob had performed an exceptionally tricky putt on the golf course. One-Armed Bob strode over and clamped his *Iron Fist of the Afterlife* onto Nathan's shoulder and said, "What did you think of the Mini-Gun kid?" He then slapped Nathan on the back good-naturedly. This caused Nathan to slide a good three feet to the left by Bob's show of camaraderie.

Nathan winced as little as he dared, trying to be as 'manly' as possible in this ultimate bastion of manliness. He squared up his shoulders and said, "Loud."

One-Armed Bob burst out with laughter. Jericho joined him. Combined, it became so overbearing that Nathan's eardrums rang like a six-foot tuning fork. He quickly clamped his jaws shut in the fear that his fillings would vibrate out and onto the floor. The fillings, however, held fast — a testament to his dentist's craftsmanship. The cacophony of mirth mercifully ended.

One-Armed Bob smiled broadly at Nathan. Nathan looked behind himself and then returned the smile. One-Armed Bob said, "Wanna arm wrestle?"

Nathan's mind reeled. He was now lost in burly man/jock country and did not have a map. He had seen his brother in many of these tense, testosterone-fueled one-up man-ships. What was the worst thing he could say? That was usually what the recipient of these farces wanted to hear. His upper brain started up on its tired logic bit when the lower brain shouted it down with *I got this*. His eyes darted down in horror seeing his mouth open by itself. It said, "Wanna lose, tin man!?" His eyes then watched as his own arms shot out and up in a double bicep pose. The arms were somewhat uncomfortable at it, never having done that before.

"Okay, kid, I know when to cut bait!" One-Armed Bob said as they stood facing each other in manliness.

Jericho was wide open mouth stunned never having seen his brother do any of these sorts of things, but decided it had to stop before Nathan blew it and started quoting Disraeli, Kierkegaard, or some other dead guy. He cleared his throat and said, "Sorry about the electrocution thing, man."

One-Armed Bob held out the *Iron Fist of Destruction* palm up and said, "It's okay. I did the same thing myself, first time 'round. I thought, what could an additional 110 volts do? Grounded, ungrounded, who cared? Just words. Well, *words have consequences*, I'm here to witness. But hey, you got a new 'doo and I got more juice for my buddy, the *Iron Fist of Doom*." He flexed his fist and it rotated 360 degrees at the wrist and said, "Feels good. Real good." He made a mouth shape with his iron thumb and index finger. He placed this 'mouth' next to his flesh and blood hand. He pivoted the thumb up and down as if it were speaking. One-Armed Bob started his ventriloquist bit, 'speaking' through his pursed lips, saying, "Hey pitiful arm! Who's the boss?! Huh?! That's right — ME!"

One-Armed Bob then separated his hands saying to them, "Break it up, you two!" And then to the iron hand, "I'm the one in charge of this bag of bones, kiddo!" The metal hand changed to a choking position and slowly made its way to One-Armed Bob's throat. One-Armed Bob snapped at it, "Just try it! A one-way ticket to the recycling bin! We have what you call a, uh, umm —?" He shot a questioning glance at Nathan.

"Symbiotic relationship," Nathan said directly to the metal fist. The iron relaxed and tipped to Nathan as if nodding. It then returned to One-Armed Bob's side.

One-Armed Bob relaxed and said to Jericho, "You're right. Lots of good words. I guess reading isn't a total waste of time."

"Perhaps only a partial waste," Nathan offered.

The iron fist lunged out at Nathan like a pit bull. One-Armed Bob popped it with his real hand as if chastising an unruly puppy.

"Hey man, we got 'ta hit the road and get at this Beast thing," Jericho said and slapped One-Armed Bob's back. "What do you have in mind? What could be better than the amazing Mini-Gun?"

One-Armed Bob, on being asked any opinion on any killing machine brightened and shifted on his feet like an excited schoolboy. He quickly went to a device shrouded with a heavy, itchy-looking Soviet-era navy blanket. "Its purpose," he paused dramatically and gripped the scratchy blanket with his metal fist and whipped it off with a snap that was as loud as a champagne cork. With a flourish, it swished around his shoulders like a cape. This allowed both hands to be free to sweep out in a grand gesture as he intoned, "*Is to kill whales.*"

The brothers Kavillehogg moaned in unison, "Whoa!"

Before them stood a mannequin, with a large backpack strapped to its back. Held between its hands was what looked like a tremendous 1950s iron vacuum cleaner. Poking out of its snout was the unmistakable double-barbed shaft of a harpoon. It was big. Big like the rear axle of a station wagon big.

The Kavillehoggs couldn't take it. Their four arms reached out and they slumped toward it, looking like extremely fresh zombies.

One-Armed Bob was prepared this time and lunged behind the mannequin, his cape flapping behind him. He stopped and yanked a large lever on the backpack downward. He straightened and said, "Please feel free to fondle the Arm of Zeus. Now that the safety is engaged — for *your* safety of course. We can't be too careful when Kavillehoggs are around."

Nathan shook his head as if clearing it and said to the mannequin, "I, as a matter of principle, don't like the killing of aquatic mammals, but, gosh, I'm, well, overwhelmed right now." He addressed Jericho, "*Now* I'm confident in the plan to end all plans."

The brothers roughly embraced like two Russian Cossacks.

One-Armed Bob put his hands on his hips as tears welled up in his eyes, nodded, and said, "Weapons of death always bring a family together." One-Armed Bob quickly got a grip on his emotions — an iron-tight grip one might say — and motioned for them to follow. In the back corner of the secret, secret armory was an eight-foot square on the floor cordoned off by a black and yellow striped area around it. He corralled the brothers into the square and slammed the *Iron Fist of the Apocalypse* onto a huge red emergency button there. Several rotating police lights lowered from the ceiling and an air raid klaxon wailed. One-Armed Bob shouted, "Brace yourselves!" The brothers, seeing nothing to brace themselves with, turned back-to-back samurai style and interlocked elbows.

The platform then descended slowly.

Very slowly.

ONE-ARMED BOB'S SECRET, SECRET, SECRET LAIR

THIRTEEN AND A HALF MINUTES LATER, the platform descended *ten feet* to the basement. The brothers had reverted to sitting cross-legged, rolling a live grenade between them, having decided better to die that way than from say, boredom. The air raid klaxon and police lights had reset and retracted themselves some time ago. The silence made the ordeal even more tedious — if that were possible. The platform finally stopped.

Nathan painfully stood, his legs having fallen asleep during the descent. He returned the grenade to One-Armed Bob and said, "I don't feel it is necessary to have passengers 'brace themselves.' I believe we had time to work the London Times crossword puzzle — Sunday edition."

One-Armed Bob was abashed. He said, "I know kid. When it was installed the floor, well, *dropped away* from under you. My girlfriend rode it once. Once. She said if I didn't slow it down she wouldn't make my buffalo chicken wings anymore. What can you do?" He clambered off toward a wall covered in photos and said over his shoulder, "The whole 'brace yourself' thing is just habit." He stopped in front of a wall covered with hundreds of very blurry black-and-white images of what could be sympathetically described as "amateur photographs." Each was attached to one another by hundreds of strings. The maze of string was overly ornate, as if a spider with anxiety issues had spun it.

Some might describe it as a methodical and scientific two-dimensional thought chart. The rest, however, would call it a jumbled mess.

The brothers exchanged a brief glance at each other and returned their gaze to this cross-stitcher's nightmare. Nathan squinted and walked close to what appeared to be a toddler's drawing of a dinosaur with a hammer-shaped head. It was done with purple and yellow Crayons. The drawing was made just above what appeared to be an upside-down monster truck.

One-Armed Bob came close, jabbed an iron

thumb at the drawing, and said, "Reliable eyewitness drawing. All he could find in his rental car was a monster trucks coloring book and two crayons. Big-time irony and all, drawing a monster over a picture of a monster truck."

Jericho piped up, "Who was this reliable witness?"

One-Armed Bob turned, grabbed what appeared to be the largest three-ring binder on Earth, and allowed his metal fingers to ruffle through several hundred pages quickly. He said, "Ah, um, oh yes, Professor Portsmouth."

Nathan's jaw drooped as he returned to the picture. He said, "But this illustration is *dreadful*."

One-Armed Bob slammed the binder closed, and tossed it to the shelf. He ripped some paper out of a spiral notebook, grabbed a grease pencil, threw them at Nathan, and demanded, "Dog. Miniature Pomeranian. Draw it! Now!" One-Armed Bob snapped his metal fingers with ultra-human speed inches from Nathan's face. Nathan dropped to his hands and knees and started scribbling. Four and a half seconds later One-Armed Bob barked, "Time's up!" and snatched the paper. One-Armed Bob looked and couldn't suppress a laugh.

The rendering of a miniature Pomeranian under

duress was a wobbly circle, four uneven stick legs, and the words 'woof-woof' above it.

"Didn't want to freak you out like that but almost no one draws even remotely well, even under good circumstances. So ease up on the prof, okay?" One-Armed Bob said and crushed the drawing into a ball smaller than a thumb tack.

Nathan was clearly pleased to see his drawing disappear so handily. He asked, "Out of curiosity, when did you see him last?"

"Two days ago."

"Why was he here?" Nathan said, trying to contain his excitement. It was his first Q&A to actually turn up useful information.

"Oh, he bought the other Mini-Gun," One-Armed Bob said and grimaced, "apparently, it wasn't enough firepower. He never came back for his deposit."

Nathan and Jericho stared at One-Armed Bob and didn't blink for a long time.

One-Armed Bob made a flourish toward the ceiling and said, "Perhaps you'll find better luck with the 'Arm of Zeus'".

The brothers said, "Jeeze Louise."

AN INTERLUDE HARDLY EVEN
WORTH MENTIONING

WITH THE 'ARM OF ZEUS' somewhat safely stowed in the back of the Taco Shack's trailer, Nathan ground several gears to powder before any forward momentum was achieved.

"Told ya. Not hard at all," Jericho commented.

Nathan, never having driven a *pick up truck*, much less an eighteen wheeler with a twelve non-synchronized gear transmission, wiped sweat from his eyes as the massive vehicle lurched forward. It was as if some giant were shaking the truck like a cheap maraca.

"But go easy, man. This thing's gotta be returned, ya know," Jericho said and instantly regretted it.

Nathan ground two more gears. The truck shuddered a bit faster now. Nathan laughed and shouted over the din as he pointed at the speedometer, "Check it out! Eighth gear and going over twenty now! I *am* getting a feel for this entire 'truckin' thing."

Jericho relaxed a bit. Perhaps Nathan wouldn't ask...

"About this truck. Are we renting it, or is it more or less, well, stolen?" Nathan said.

Jericho now shifted a bit. This of course was lost in the rocking and shuddering of Nathan's 'truckin'.

Jericho tried a pondering look on for size and realized it *just didn't fit*. He said, "Well, Ariolano said we could borrow it to get another car from, from uh, *home?*" His 'rascal brain' was busy looking deep in its file cabinet of excuses trying to get a good one lined up for Nathan's next question. It had just opened the bottom drawer when —.

Nathan said, "Why don't we just skip six or seven gears and get to the fast and fun ones?"

The truck was well built, but not to Kavillehogg tolerances. A pole of metal resembling a t-ball stand shot through the hood of the truck and flew end over end and into a grove of trees. The engine groaned as if it had been punched in the gut, which, in mechanical terms it had been. A column of flame burst out of the hole.

"WHOA!!!" the brothers cheered, then looked about, remembering this wasn't their truck.

"I know less than nothing about internal combustion engines. I want to know what you think that was. I, however, really, I, but, but, *but just look at that flame!*" Nathan said, his eyes widening, not with fear but excitement. His inner pyromaniac was rubbing its hands gleefully.

Jericho's inner pyro was sloshing gasoline around the inside of his skull and flicking the cover of its lighter open and closed manically. Jericho's eyes were locked onto the beautiful orange and blue shaft of fire. His cheeks flushed. His nostrils flared. He reached out to touch the oh-so-pretty flame but luckily the windshield arrested his movement.

Which was just as well, because his brother was trying to do the same. They resembled toddlers in front of an aquarium filled with shiny guppies. They were transfixed with awe.

Nathan leaned forward again to touch the dancing fire. In doing so, he depressed the gas pedal. This in turn caused the flame to shoot thirty-two feet straight up. The brothers lost the gift of speech at this spectacle and started to grunt like crazed apes while hopping up and down. Even apes, however, would have realized the danger and shown the good sense to turn off the motor. The brother's good sense, on the other hand, had descended to the root cellar of their lower brain and was beginning to dig.

The hood of the truck started to glow dirty orange and then became an attractive shade of bright red. Nathan's good sense had hit bedrock now and had started to watch funny cat videos on the internet. He jammed the gas pedal to the floor so hard it stuck there. The truck's moan turned to a cacophony of screeches as the engine bowed and said, "I'm outta here," and then exploded. The hood roared off into the sky along with the engine as a six-foot-wide column of burning fuel followed it, like a moonshot from the 1960s.

Jericho's eyes actually bugged out of his skull and he shouted over the explosion, "KILL ME NOW, 'CAUSE EVERYTHING AFTER THIS WILL FEEL LIKE CHEAP CORNBREAD DRESSING!!!"

The brothers leapt down from the truck and stared upward as the flaming engine thundered up into the stratosphere.

Moments later, several military jets roared after it, afterburners at full, just trying to keep up. It quickly became quiet.

"I thought it may be a *lark* — you know — *fun*

being a detective. But well, this is, *thrilling*," Nathan said and turned to his brother for a reaction. Jericho only pointed to the receding fire in the sky. Nathan patted Jericho gently on the head and they walked around the completely ruined, soot-covered truck cabin and toward the rear end of its metallic, heat-buckled trailer.

RETRIEVING THE ARM OF ZEUS

JERICHO HOPPED up and wrenched open the back of the truck's trailer. Snuggled between several hundred sacks of masa flour and cumin was the 'Arm of Zeus'. It was so heavy even Jericho had to use both hands to carry it down from the trailer. He said, "Man, this thing is made to last!"

The backpack was labeled in Russian Cyrillic lettering, which, when translated read 'Tremendous stored inertia /Do not jostle or shake/Extremely dangerous.' Jericho could not read Russian however and he slung the backpack of the device onto his back with Jericho-like bravado. The straps were adjusted to a regular sized person however, and it fell to the ground and made a sound which was creepily like a horse whinnying. Like a cheap radio controlled car it vibrated, rattled and turned in a tight circle. Jericho, with Jericho-like disregard kicked it as hard as he could and shouted, "I'm the boss of you!" The pack whinnied once more and stopped. He shook his finger at the device and then strapped it on, picking up the enormous twin handled harpoon and laid it against his shoulder like a rifle.

Nathan pointed and said, "You know generally, as a rule, I don't go for the whole 'manly' bit, but you look about 135 percent awesome wearing that thing."

Although Jericho's bodybuilder bearing doesn't allow for him to stand any taller, he did extend his neck upward to allow him to be that wee bit higher. The brothers smiled at one another.

"I guess we walk back," Jericho said and strode down the road.

THEY HAD GONE ABOUT three miles in when a military Hum Vee passed them, turned hard, and tore up the road's blacktop as it pulled up to them and stopped. The windows were tinted so dark as to appear painted black. It just sat there as if saying, "Ain't I great?"

Nathan started to whisper out of the corner of

his mouth, which was completely unnecessary as the Humvee was as loud as a classroom of third graders. No one inside it could hear Nathan even if they tried. And the glass was so dark, they couldn't read his lips, either. He said, "I guess the military wasn't so happy with our moon shot."

Jericho shifted the harpoon from his shoulder to his hand and countered, "Wanna test this baby out?"

Nathan blanched.

"I'm kidding little brother," Jericho said.

The window rolled slowly down. From the darkness, a voice boomed out, "Hey kid, wanna piece of candy?!" An ear-splitting laugh erupted from the Humvee's darkness. An odd metal clank sounded and One-Armed Bob's head poked out and smiled, "I was listening to the military radio bands. They thought they had a UFO on their hands. Grabbed a camera and had 'ta check it out. Shoulda known a Kavillehogg was behind these shenanigans! Better climb aboard, the real men in black will be here soon."

Jericho smiled and said, "Bob, you're my one winged guardian angel!" Both manly men boomed laughter at each other. This carried on for several minutes.

Nathan was now terrified that the men in black

were coming and gently pushed Nathan to the side so he could clamber up into the big military transport. Jericho punched his own gut several times to ease a cramp that was rearing its ugly head there. He tossed the fragile inertia backpack into the rear and, just for kicks, rode on the sideboard of the Humvee like a secret service agent. Whenever the Humvee passed anything living he put his hand to his ear and hollered over the road noise, "We have President Kavillehogg in transport to the White House, over!" Both he and One-Armed Bob found this side split-tingly funny the entire trip back into town.

Nathan was slouched down so that no one would see him — which was ironic in that no one could see him through the dark atomic blast glass even if they wanted to.

A black windowless van with government tags roared past them in the opposite direction. It was filled with grown men in black suits and wearing what appeared to be old-style welder's goggles, the ones with individual leather cups for each eye.

One-Armed Bob was eating whole coffee beans out of a bag in the front seat by the handful, chasing them with shots of boiling hot water. Through this hot mush, he said, "Told ya kid, they *always* show up." He looked directly at Jericho, and pointed to the back of the Humvee at the 'Arm of Zeus'. "You can't throw that thing around. It's jammed to the gills with what's called stored inertia. That's what engineer types say when they mean a bunch of something. In this case inertia, or, energy. Enough energy to put that harpoon through a whale, or, the hull of your own ship depending on how bad your aim is. It's really dangerous. Says so on the backpack, kapisch?"

Jericho raised an eyebrow and said, "I knew it was in *Chinese*! They make everything, you know?" He was overwhelmed with all the knobs and gadgets on the dashboard of the Humvee. Unknowingly, he leaned through the window to pull on an especially stout lever. One-Armed Bob was watching him and popped him with the *Iron Fist of Discipline*. Jericho yelped and put his hand in his mouth.

"Sorry kids, but ya gotta stop touching stuff. You'll never make it to thirty. My secret and secret, secret lairs are a wreck because of you two," One-Armed Bob said, his face turning a light shade of crimson.

"About that secret, secret lair. I was curious about your insurance coverage," Nathan said.

One-Armed Bob laughed and laughed. He eventually stopped and wiped his nose with his sleeve. He caught a breath and said, "They don't issue insurance coverage for giant machine guns and Soviet rocket launchers. Look, you just owe me a smallish suitcase full of money. Period."

Nathan squirmed a bit thinking about the dinging sound his debit card made when he last tried to use it to buy some thirty-cent snack cakes. He managed to say, "Is that stuff legal? I mean it is hidden not only in a back room, but a secret, secret lair."

It was One-Armed Bob's turn to squirm. He said offhandedly, "It's not *really*, well, I guess technically it *is*. But not according to our constitution, you know. You used to be able to buy a fully automatic Tommy Gun *through the mail*. From *department stores*! But, saying that out loud I admit, I do sleep better at night knowing that not everyone can get their hands on one. I was a decorated Army Ranger though, so I at least *I* know what I'm doing. Usually. Seventy-eight percent of the time — tops."

Nathan straightened a bit and said, "So, all that stuff is stolen?!"

"*Stolen* is a strong word. Perhaps on *loan* from several different nation's fine armories. Most of it was collecting dust. My having the 'Arm of Zeus' is saving the lives of countless whales," One-Armed Bob said and brightened at the thought.

"But you sell them," Nathan said, trying to wrap his head around this double talk and, at the same time, not wanting to lose this ride into town.

"That's not entirely true, young man. In the store, everything to the rear of the 'Knives of Certain and Excruciating Death' cabinet is *for loan*, if that makes you feel better. It should. However, you two, in the span of seven minutes destroyed almost all of it, so what difference does it make? Also, I only loan them out to fine citizens like yourselves. What are you going to go up against the Bayou Beast with your local Made in China Megastore? I mean *really*. A .22 dolled up to look like an M-16? What I provide may not be *legal* but in your case sure is *necessary*. Look, if you should come across some dough in this case of yours, spread some of it my way. At least enough to plaster over the 23,761 holes in the ceiling, walls, and floor. Most importantly, my snack vending machine. It's ruined. All the sticky bun's little plastic bags were perforated — they're all stale now," One-Armed Bob's eyes welled with tears.

Jericho reached over and gripped One-Armed Bob's shoulder and gave it a gentle squeeze. One-

Armed Bob nodded and brushed aside the tears with an iron finger.

"I am truly sorry about the sticky buns, Bob. And if we get out of this with some, um, *dough* as you say, you will receive a portion. In order to do that, we need to be transported to the bayou to retrieve our client's father," Nathan said.

"*Father?* I hate to break it to you, as a detective and all, but Professor Portsmouth doesn't have kids, and," One-Armed Bob said, "he's single-pingle."

The brothers exchanged a look. Jericho decided that the look was achieving nothing and shrugged his shoulders instead.

"Why do you surmise that the professor is childless? Or single for that matter?" Nathan said.

"Easy cheese, detective man. A, he doesn't have any grey hair — ergo, he has no children. B, he told me that he enjoyed sitting on his couch in his underwear eating baked beans out of the can while watching ladies mud wrestling — he is most definitely not married," One-Armed Bob said and made a flourish with his *Iron Fist of Truth*.

"How did you come up with this data about his — eating habits?" Nathan asked, almost stuttering.

"Oh, I told him about my girlfriend telling, no,

demanding I slow down my superhero-esque freight platform and the whole no chicken wings threat. He, in turn, told me about his baked beans/couch setup. Said he was unattached, never married, and can do anything he wanted, whenever he wanted... whenever he wanted..." One-Armed Bob muttered and his eyes became distant, unfocused. The Humvee swerved a bit before One-Armed Bob got it under control.

"Hey sorry kids, I was having one of those lucid dream thingies," One-Armed Bob said.

"I don't know about this case, little brother, it is getting *weird*," Jericho said and watched the retreating men in the black van in the rearview mirror.

A long moment passed. The Humvee's massive wheels continued making their bee-like humming sound.

"No. It is becoming exceedingly interesting. Exceedingly," Nathan said and smiled, "Someone has tried to take advantage of the Kavillehoggs. I will not allow this to happen. One-Armed Bob, turn this farcically large car around and bring us to the Bayou."

Jericho wasn't used to his brother showing initiative of any sort. Asking for salt *and then for pepper* was a bold day for Nathan. He asked his brother, "You feeling okay, man?"

Nathan sat higher in his chair and said, "Yes, I really am. I am experiencing self-confidence. Let's take advantage of it while it lasts. One-Armed Bob, I understand this vehicle can perform a one hundred-and-eighty-degree turn without slowing. I do not think it can. *Prove it.*"

One-Armed Bob yelled, "Sua Sponte!" This is the US Army Ranger's motto — it is Latin for 'Of their own accord'. His iron fist then acted of its own accord and wrenched the wheel to the left with all its strength. The Humvee was doing 65 miles per hour.

PHYSICS VERSUS ONE-ARMED BOB

LIKE A SPILLING PLATE of sausages that a lap dog had been eyeing greedily, things happened rather quickly.

A two-foot long tungsten steel spike shot straight down into the cringing asphalt. A ninety-foot, 300,000-pound-test-strength cable quickly unspooled. Having reached its end, at which a ten-foot steel spring was attached, the forward motion of the Humvee was completely halted. The result was that the spring became, momentarily, a *stored inertia machine.* Unlike the 'Arm of Zeus' however, the stored inertia was instantaneously released in the opposite direction. The 7,700-pound vehicle was slingshot *backward* at 65 miles per hour. Like a Navy fighter jet ripping off the deck of an aircraft carrier, the passengers were plastered to their seats by the incredible g-forces. This did not, however, deter Jericho and One-Armed Bob from whooping and hollering *faster* than the speed of sound.

Many would argue that one cannot defeat the laws of physics in this manner. However, when it came down to physics versus One-Armed Bob, physics generally lost.

Jericho however, lost to physics and his tight 'fro was straightened out by the incredible g-forces. He later admitted that though his hair in fact looked phenomenal, tight curls weren't really his bag.

The cable reached its end and was released. The Humvee's being slingshot actually had it airborne for forty-two seconds. It skipped twice, landed, and One-Armed Bob made excellent time on the way to the Wholly Magnificent Swamp Bayou Air Boat Ride.

A SOMEWHAT TRIUMPHANT RETURN TO THE WHOLLY MAGNIFICENT BAYOU AIRBOAT RIDE

THE HUMMER WASN'T EVEN STOPPED when Jericho kicked the door open, rolled out, and ran to the proprietor of the airboat ride. He grabbed the proprietor and carried him back to the now-parked Hummer. Jericho stuck the proprietor's head into the combat vehicle's open window.

In the Hummer's driver seat, One-Armed Bob raised the *Iron Fist of Ultimate Driving Skill* and uncurled a single metal finger which he pointed at the proprietor's goggling eyes. One-Armed Bob said, "Are you listening?" The proprietor's eyes goggled even more. One-Armed Bob was well pleased and said, "Good. These boys have to find someone in the bayou who has been abducted."

"Or eaten!" said the proprietor, his fear of the

Bayou Beast trumping that of a man with a bionic arm. But not by much — his fear caused his own upper dentures to fly out of his mouth and they plopped down into Bob's real hand. One-Armed Bob cringed ever so slightly as the wet slapping sound reached his ears.

From the back seat, Nathan gagged. His mild case of self-esteem had fled at the sight of the saliva-soaked flying teeth.

One-Armed Bob said, "Listen, you are the only one who can steer that floating death trap and by gum, *you will*." He glanced down at the pool of saliva in which the denture sat, and, fighting the urge to throw up said, "I've plucked beating hearts out of men's chests and fed it to them but I flat out refuse to put these fake teeth back in your mouth. Why don't you reach down and put them back yourself? They're about to float out of my palm all on their own."

From the back seat was heard, "Great gobbly-goo-ga!"

Both the proprietor and One-Armed Bob turned to look at Nathan. One-Armed Bob said, "Don't mind him, he's had a trying day. But you Captain, you are bringing these kids out to help them finish their mission. And get these teeth. My skin is starting to prune." With a shaking hand, the proprietor returned the teeth to his mouth and jiggled his jaw back and forth. This created a dreadful sucking/bubbling noise.

From the back seat came some serious gagging.

One-Armed Bob flung his hand down and slung the spit onto the rubber floor mat of the Hummer. Nathan could only hear the wet slap of the saliva wad. This was, of course, more than anyone sane was supposed to deal with, and promptly threw up straight over the back seat and into the proprietor's open mouth. This triggered an in-vehicle vomit party. As these parties tend to be short-lived, it was soon quiet.

Those who could understand the language of machines would have heard the Hummer say, "Yucka-doo and Tigger too!"

One-Armed Bob, being part machine, heard the combat vehicle's lament and patting the dash said, "It's okay big boy, I'll hose you out soon as we get away from these nasty people."

He wiped his own puke-covered chin with the *Iron Fist of Utter Distain* and then pushed the proprietor's head out of the front seat. Then he jabbed a smelly iron thumb toward the back seat and ordered, "You. Out. And good luck kid. Jericho, grab the Arm of Zeus."

Jericho had barely gotten the harpoon out when One-Armed Bob dropped it in first and peeled out, covering the trio in dust.

"That man *got issues*," the proprietor said and trudged toward the airboat.

Jericho turned to Nathan, sniffed, and said, "That wedding cake icing smells good going down, but pure-d-nasty coming back up."

Nathan, vomit-exhausted, said, "I concur," and trudged off to the boat.

Jericho easily slung the 'Arm of Zeus' inertia pack over his shoulder, grabbed the harpoon, and strode to the now idling airboat. Next to the dock, Nathan was sitting by the proprietor, muttering apologies.

THE WHOLE HEART 'A DARKNESS THINGY

THE AIRBOAT SKIMMED over the placid brown water of the bayou, herons and other skittish birds swooping out of its way. The proprietor did a very fancy pants spin with the airboat causing it to do a one-hundred-and-eighty-six-degree turn. This effectively stopped their forward momentum and the boat just sat there, as if waiting on a factory rebate for a washer/drier combo which it knew instinctively would never arrive but patiently awaited nonetheless.

The proprietor looked about and said quietly, "Do you think that fella with the steel hook can hear us?"

Nathan, who was under the proprietor and tightly gripping the base of the man's tower/seat said,

"I believe it is a hand, and he said it's made out of iron."

Jericho chimed in with, "You wouldn't believe the things he can do with that thing, it's like —"

The proprietor held his hand up, "Look, I know you two got something against the Bayou Beast but I don't. That's that whole heart a' darkness thingy. Goin' out in the back bayou is just stupid. And dumb."

Nathan's inner grammar teacher clawed its way to the surface of his consciousness and said, "Actually, the additional 'dumb' wasn't necessary as you had already said 'stupid.' This clearly contradicts and almost negates your verbal posture."

The proprietor frowned, perceptibly straightened his back, and said, "Looky, what I mean is that we can't do squat. I don't know what your mission is and don't wanna, okay?"

Nathan said from the base of the chair, "Looky, um, excuse me, I mean look, we need to get out to find the Bayou Beast and — kill it. We think it may have eaten the father of our client and he may still be alive in the belly of the beast. Oh, I've always loved that phrase! The belly of the beast. Yes. *Anyway!* We have a good weapon and my brother is very strong." From his side-lying position he yanked a hand free of the seat's base and motioned to his brother.

Jericho turned to show the backpack with the Russian stenciling and smiled. Jericho tipped his head to the pack and said, "It's just chock full of *stored inertia*. Point this harpoon thing at the beast, and all that *stored inertia* is released and the pointy part goes faster than a NASCAR slap into the beast. Then we cut the beast open and scoot on home. It's kinda the plan to end all plans, you know?"

The proprietor squinted and said, "Ya had me believing this up to — *faster than a NASCAR*. Ain't nothin' faster than a NASCAR! Anyway, don't you have to tie something to connect the harpoon thingy to this boat? Otherwise, it's like throwing a fish hook and line over the side without being tied to the fishing pole. Right?"

Nathan saw his chance to bring the proprietor in on the plan to end all plans. He pointed to the proprietor and said, "That is brilliant! No, wait. *You are brilliant.* If we didn't do that the beast would get away! I'm so glad you came along. Tell us your idea about how to connect this vessel to the harpoon's projectile barb."

The proprietor had never heard the combination of the words *you* and *brilliant* in the same sentence.

It was a galvanizing experience and he was instantly sold on this plan. He said, "Well, we take, say, this line." He bent over and picked up the rope he used to anchor the airboat for fishing and alligator hunting charters. "And tie it to the hasp on the bottom of the pointy part of the barb thingy. It's a bit short. Uh, well, maybe that ain't such a hot idea after all —"

Jericho heard the familiar words — uh, well, maybe — and knew he was listening to a kindred soul. He cut the proprietor short with his standard response which was, "It'll be fine." He shrugged, smiled, and said, "Short line? No problem. We just get close. Real close. So close we feel its hot breath on our faces, see what it had for dinner stuck in its teeth!"

Nathan was standing now. He and the proprietor grabbed each other in fright, their mouths a straight line, and said in unison, "Yeeesh!"

"Man up boys, this is something we can brag about in the old folks home fifty years from now!" Jericho said.

When they were done yammering, a twenty-three-foot alligator clambered into the airboat.

Pandemonium ensued.

AN UNINVITED GUEST

TWO THINGS HAPPENED AT ONCE.

First, Nathan leapt up and into the proprietor's arms. This made the proprietor look like one of those bodybuilders that carry around a Chihuahua.

Second, Jericho spun around and immediately went into a sumo wrestler pose. He had been waiting all his life to wrestle an alligator.

The alligator saw this and became uneasy about the situation. Only moments before, he had smelled a dead body, probably a really big juicy bloated one by the sheer power of the stink's ability to penetrate that deep into the water. Usually, humans wet their pants and literally ran across the surface of the water to the shore. Now though, he was up against an admittedly big dude, but one who had watched far too many bad safari movies. Humans have trouble enough standing upright in a bayou's mucky muck, much less trying to wrestle with a reptile that is four hundred pounds and all muscle. And teeth. *A whole lot of teeth*, the alligator thought to himself and shook his giant head the inch or two left and right that his short neck would allow. He was jarred from his musings as the overpowering stench smacked his green nostrils again. *Yum*, he thought, *delicious dead bodies*. Like the Kavillehogg brothers, the alligator's stomach had total control over all other systems in its body, even those of survival. It turned to the dead bodies. The alligator blinked twice — one of the humans had apparently died in that silly standing upright position they liked so much. To top the bill, another had died curled up in the other's arms. Their shirts were smeared with green slime. *What in the heck is going on in this boat?* He thought. But they were dead for sure, they hadn't even breathed since he turned toward them. They sure smelled good though — *really putrescent, gotta eat me some of that!* The alligator trudged toward them on his stumpy legs when his forward motion stopped. He looked down and saw his clawed feet going back and forth but the deck wasn't moving. *Oh man*, the alligator thought, *the wrestler! Stomach, you are in ten kinds of trouble!* For the first time in his long life, he experienced the sensation of flying. He didn't care for it.

Jericho had taken the tail of the alligator and started to spin it around and around. The alligator's eyes crossed and its four stumpy legs curled in toward its tummy. It then sprayed a circular arc of very long dead animal vomit. This rained down on everyone, grossing out Jericho who then let go of the alligator. It spun away in a wide green blur through the humid air.

Typical thought the alligator as it spun downward, toward the bayou. It struck the water at about thirty miles an hour and skipped upon the surface of the water for not one, but six skips, stopping at the edge of the water where several lady alligators were quietly sunning themselves. Their startled expression turned to one of admiration. Though the alligator was dizzy as all get out, he noticed their looks and showed a toothy grin. They tittered. He winked, gave a very broad smile, and said, *Good afternoon, ladies.*

THE PROPRIETOR BAILS OUT

THE PROPRIETOR'S left eye started twitching. He quivered a bit. He straightened, pivoted, and set Nathan, who was still curled up in a ball, onto the driver's seat atop the pedestal. He brushed himself off and reached into a storage locker. He grabbed a rusty machete and, underneath everything, his never-used life vest. He had to tug to break it free of the mildew growing along the bottom of the locker. The vest had the word Captain emblazoned across its back in glittery cursive letters but was barely legible because of the coating of black mold. He snapped it like a whip upward and created what looked like a small black thundercloud over the boat. It drifted down and stuck to everyone's human and alligator vomit-crusted clothes. They looked as if they had been fried, salted, and peppered.

Jericho, befuddled, watched the proprietor who now looked like a sprightly thrift store shopper, eagerly choosing one worn-out item after another. Then Jericho's nose scrunched and realized it was his nasty shirt. He said, "Man, I *stink*. What do gators eat? I mean. I *really* smell. Say, in that locker thingy do you have any, I don't know, bayou airboat t-shirts, or, hey yeah — *any muscle shirts?* After hurling that gator into the next world, I gotta pretty tight pump going on." He then flexed his left forearm which split his shirt sleeve like a ripe banana, and said in a girly voice, "Whoops! However did that happen? Hey proprietor, what's the similarity between me and Janet Jackson?"

The proprietor stopped rummaging and stood upright saying, "I honestly don't know."

Jericho raised his unscathed right sleeve, flexed his arm, and destroyed the fabric. He put his pinky to his chin, looked coy, and said, "We are both having costume malfunctions!" He then laughed so loud that a nearby gang of Herons decided then and there that *now, right now*, was the best time to fly south for the winter, and in a huff, the flock cleared out of the bayou.

"You are, by yourself, destroying this here ecosystem!" the proprietor said after removing his fingers from his ears, "I had my pinkies jammed in my ears up to the knuckle and they're still ringing." He bent over the locker and using his rusty machete as a pry bar, got his 1986 Motorola cellular phone broken loose from where it had rusted onto the boat like a metal barnacle. The phone looked like a low-tech lunch box with an old-style telephone handset poking out of the top with the curled wire attaching it to the side of the transmitter/lunchbox doohickey. It looked heavy as he slung it over his lifejacket. He looked about sadly and patted the airplane motor.

Nathan, who was wakened — along with the rest of the southeastern United States — by Jericho's bellow was eyeing the proprietor warily. Unlike his mildly sociopathic brother, Nathan had bags of empathy and the proprietor's actions and facial gestures had him worried. Like an Italian grandmother seeing a child not eat five helpings of her tortellini, he knew something was badly wrong. He said quietly, "Um, er, are you going to, well, abandon ship?"

"Sir, I can barely hear," the proprietor said, throwing a thumb toward Jericho who was now tying the shards of his sleeves into multiple granny knots,

"Someone keeps firing that Howitzer." The proprietor glanced to the nearby shore. He said, "Look, I got nothing against either of ya, but you boys are ten kinds of crazy. Crazy people get sane people killed. And you're battier than my gym teacher — 'nuff said." Smiling, the proprietor leapt into the water and waded toward the shore.

"COME BACK!!!" Nathan shrieked, his eyeballs trying to jump out of his head.

As the proprietor doggy paddled, he shouted over his shoulder, "There's enough gas in her to get you to the moon and back. Keep heading south to where that company has been trying to drain the back bayou. The Beast has destroyed most of their really heavy equipment. Chewed it up and spit it out." He made it to the shore and turned. Jericho was on the deck, one foot planted on the driver's pedestal, hands on his hips — like in some madman's idea of an underwear ad. Jericho nodded sagely and gave the proprietor a crisp salute.

"Yeah, okay, gotta run," the proprietor said and ran into the thick jungle foliage, macheteing his way through it like a berserker. With the exception of the flock of Heron's wings fading in the distance, the bayou was really, really quiet.

"We are in serious trouble. I don't want to die in

the bayou. To be perfectly candid, I don't want to die at all," Nathan said, to no one in particular.

Jericho spit high into the air and then caught it in his mouth again. He reached up and easily lifted his brother's curled-up body out of the driver's chair and set him down behind the pedestal. He patted the curled form and said, "Ain't nobody gonna die today. I'm in charge of this rust bucket and now we are gonna see what this baby can really do!" He grabbed the tiller with one hand and shoved the starter button so hard it shot out sparks. The engine roared to life. A devilish look flashed into Jericho's eyes. He revved the big motor over and over.

"How can you be certain no one is going — to die?" Nathan whimpered and looked about the bayou with increasing unease.

Jericho tapped his brother's head with his dangling foot. Nathan glanced up, looking just pitiful.

Jericho winked and said, "Because little brother, *I said so.*" He then laughed and jammed the throttle as far as it would go and then shoved it some more, bending the thick metal shaft for good measure.

FAR ABOVE, the Heron's flock closed into an easily maintained V pattern. Even as the bayou quickly receded as they flew south five months early, Jericho's maniacal laughter reached them, fifteen miles away. The lead Heron looked to his wingman. They shrugged to each other, the meaning clear —
Humans, what can you do?

A TRULY UNPLEASANT SURPRISE

THE AIRBOAT WAS TEARING across the water at incredible speed. Unlike a river, bayous are incredibly twisty and turny. From the air, they look like a labyrinth designed by an ill-tempered and possibly intoxicated Franciscan Monk. Because of Jericho's insane velocity, the boat was banking left and right every twenty-seven seconds.

This made for an amazingly unnerving ride for Nathan. He chose finally, to sit directly behind the tall driver's platform and faced the rear of the boat. His view now was almost all engine, an airplane propeller and in his peripheral vision, freaked-out ducks and snakes scrambling onto the shore. He tried repeatedly to imagine himself running his fingertips along the ancient books in the Bodleian Library with its four-hundred-year-old shelves and vaulted ceiling. However, due to the real-world noise, his fine calm fantasy turned to that of a surly librarian who kept yelling at him with a thick accent about his "Bloody elephantine overdue book fine." Unfortunately, a combination of that and a paranoid image of the boat hitting an underwater stump causing him to fly face-first into the giant propeller was too much.

Nathan's eyes decided enough is enough and slammed shut with an audible whack. His shoulders, which had previously been so bunched up that they had been blocking his ears, slowly lowered. The blaring white noise of the propeller combined with the rhythmic rocking of the boat as it banked left and right lulled him to sleep.

"AGHHHHH!!!!!!"

The bloodcurdling shriek slammed Nathan's conscious into overdrive. His eyelids ripped open and then quickly slammed shut again.

His upper brain said in a somewhat stilted and unconvincing manner, *Aha, a lucid dream — a terrifyingly horrible awful dream — but a lucid dream nonetheless.*

His lower brain shoved the upper brain aside and brayed, *Shut your trap, college boy! THIS IS REAL, BABY! So, put away your fancy-pants wool jacket with the suede elbow patches. EYES, OPEN UP!*

Nathan's eyelids creaked open. Everything appeared with incredible clarity and in very slow motion. Jericho was still hollering but Nathan couldn't decide if he was in shock or speaking in tongues. The boat was spinning in a tight circle now. Jericho kept pointing up and babbling nonsense. Nathan made the fatal error of following Jericho's pointing finger.

Looming over the airboat — eighty feet tall — was the Bayou Beast.

The Bayou Beast now seemed a woefully inadequate name. Thinking about The Betty's soiled underwear, Nathan now understood. Completely. The massive rectangular hammer head pivoted down as its — *sure enough* — glowing red eyes glared down at them from each end of its huge head. A tiny part of Nathan's brain remembered that The Betty was also right on the money that this giant, giant, giant monster was almost silent. Which *did* make it even scarier — as if that was even possible. Suddenly, the Beast's jaw dropped open, twenty feet wide, and was crammed full of teeth. Hundreds of them, jagged, dripping thousand of drops of murky bayou water down onto them.

The jaw had opened all the way and the head reared up slightly.

The head, the mouth, and all its jagged teeth dropped eighty feet down onto them and everything was darkness.

NOT DEAD... YET

THE BLACK NOTHINGNESS became a little less so as dim red and blue light slowly became brighter. The airboat had been swallowed whole and was at a crazy angle now, the roar of the airplane motor made Nathan's teeth chatter so much that he started poking every button and lever he could reach.

Jericho was hanging from the driver's platform and noted that his biceps were looking pretty chiseled for a dead guy. He slowly did a pull-up and lowered himself, kissing the swollen muscles as they inflated and deflated.

"Help me over here!" Nathan tried to shout over the roar of the motor, still hitting anything mechanical he could find.

"I can't hear you over the motor! Let me turn it

off!" Jericho bellowed, his voice easily heard over the motor and probably by the citizens of Moscow. He took himself away from his private muscle pose-down and using one hand did a full pull-up to the driver's control panel and, with his free hand's pinky, hit the emergency shut-off button. The motor shuddered once and stopped.

Nathan shook his head to try to chase out the reverberating noise still clattering around in there. Satisfied, he looked about, squinting in the gloomy-colored light. He experienced a chill.

"Got this little brother!" Jericho said and clapped his hands twice.

"Come off it, that never wor —" Nathan was cut off by a blinding bank of bright white l.e.d. lights that made the inside of the Beast's 'mouth' seem like a surgical theater.

"Hey man, this isn't a mouth it's like a, a —"

"Machine," Nathan said and nodded, his hands on his hips.

"So the beast isn't real? I don't mind telling you, I was *freaked out*, but not, you know, *scared*," Jericho said and laughed nervously.

Nathan continued to look about and said, "I myself was in a blind panic. But this isn't just a machine, it's a —"

"Repurposed cargo container, young man," a deep voice said from beyond the bank of bright lights, effectively making the voice disembodied.

Jericho, who was not, you know, *scared*, jumped four feet straight up and banged his head on the ceiling of the cargo container, denting the metal. He dropped to the deck of the boat, knocked out cold. Nathan looked down at Jericho's body and shook his head.

"I shall bring an emergency first aid kit," the voice began but was waved off by Nathan.

"You would be better served by bringing a metal fitter to repair your..." Nathan said and faltered.

"The locals prefer to call it, I believe, a Bayou Beast," the voice said and sighed resignedly, it took a sharp inhalation, "I prefer The Shiva."

"The destroyer," Nathan said quietly.

There was movement behind Nathan and he spun. He was confronted by a small, frail woman in a pressed white linen suit. She held a small wireless microphone and switched it off. Her voice was now soft and quiet.

"Welcome aboard the Shiva, I believe you and I can talk at a level. It will be a welcome change," she said and looked down at Jericho's mass of flesh and muscle, "A very welcome change, indeed. He will be attended to, come with me. I believe you will like it here. We can speak more comfortably in the library."

At this, Nathan perked up and said, "*Library?*"

"Young man, do you ever go anywhere without a book?"

"Of course not — what civilized person would?"

"Precisely. Follow me, and stay close. The Shiva is something of a maze."

Nathan was led down eight flights of stairs turning left and right. Then, it seemed to him that he was traveling in a straight line. He assumed that this was the 'body' of the Beast, or, The Shiva, he corrected himself. The ship, what he had seen of it so far, was the opposite of fancy. It did seem, however, very sturdy, everything being braced and welded, he thought, to an unnecessary degree. Also, it was very bright, and though the ceilings were low, he did not feel at all claustrophobic. It was comforting in fact — like a bacon, lettuce, and tomato sandwich with what would seem to some an unnecessary amount of bacon, say perhaps ten or fifteen strips of thick-cut hickory smoked —.

He ran smack into the back of the diminutive woman. His food fantasy overrode all else, not seeing that she had stopped by a door and was almost knocked over as she was pulling out a fragile-looking key.

"Focus, young man," she managed as she regained her footing and straightened her coat.

"I am so sorry! I was thinking about food, and, well, I — wasn't focused. Please forgive me," Nathan said his head tilted almost to the floor.

The woman nodded and placed the frail key into the door's lock. She stood aside and motioned for him to enter.

Nathan paused a moment and said, "Please," motioning for her to enter the room first.

She looked from him to the doorway. She gave Nathan a brief smile and said, "I now know we will be able to speak easily to one another, as equals," her eyes glistened. "Thank you for that, I know it makes me sound as old as I am, but it is rare and beautiful when you find someone who will open a door for you, much less insist on it. Fine jewelry and estates can be bought — fine manners, young man, cannot."

Nathan was slightly embarrassed and said, "Manners are merely a series of minor inconveniences."

The woman gently poked Nathan's chest with her key and said, "No, it is a way — a manner, if you will — in which to give a small kindness to a complete stranger in an increasingly loud and brittle world. Now come along, I know you'll enjoy this," she walked through the doorway, her slight limp now more pronounced.

Nathan followed. He took in a sharp breath at what he saw.

THE BIG MAN MAKES AN APPEARANCE

HIGH ABOVE THEM IN THE 'HEAD' of the
Shiva, Jericho was wakened by a very Big Man in a
very big tan colored martial arts outfit. His Gi, the
traditional loose-fitting karate uniform, was tied at
the waist with a worn-out black belt. The Gi was, at
a minimum a XXXL. At a minimum. The Big Man
held a long beautiful wooden staff and gently nudged
Jericho with it.

Jericho smirked, grabbed the staff, and tried to
yank it free of the Big Man. Anyhow, that was his
initial plan; it was as if the staff was set in cement.
And not cheap cement either, the good stuff.
Jericho's smirk shifted to a low-grade frown and he
swung his foot out. It connected with the Big Man's
shin bone with a dull but resonant *thunk*. The Big

Man did not wince, nor did he attempt to strike back. He, like a parent with five kids, just stood there, absorbed the abuse, and did not let it bother him.

Jericho shrugged and then used the staff to pull himself up. He drew his arm back and swung as hard as he could at the center of the man's face. He allowed the punch to go wide at the last moment, whistling past the Big Man's head causing the man's hair to flutter a bit as it did. Jericho sensed he would have taken the punch many times without complaint. So, being Jericho, he did what any relatively sane man would not do. He came up close to the man, inches from his passive face. And, like a favorite aunt, pinched the man's cheek and shook it until it made a wet flarping sound. Then he said in a high-pitched voice, "You've been a *bad, bad boy!*" The man did not smile or frown. He did, however, raise his eyebrows two inches with a 'are you quite done yet' arch to them. This, for whatever reason, satisfied Jericho immensely and he put his hands to his hips like a mom about to read out the riot act. He said, "That's sharp karate Gi you got there. Be straight with me because I wasn't around at the time. But honestly, was *everyone* kung fu fighting?"

The Big Man straightened himself and then the lapels of his rather nice Gi. He said matter of factly,

"Yes." He led Jericho off the airboat and onto a shallow ledge by a large red lever. He then motioned to a yellow-striped rail above their heads and said, "Grab that rail and don't let go, this can be a bit disconcerting."

Jericho grabbed the rail and muttered, "Discon-wha?"

The Big Man jerked the red lever backward and the twenty-foot wide 'jaw' swung away from under the airboat. The boat seemed to hang in the air by itself for a moment and suddenly dropped down. It tumbled end over end until eighty feet later it struck the water nose first and stuck in the mud below. It quivered slightly like an obese arrow. The Big Man pushed the lever forward and the enormous jaw with its hundreds of jagged teeth closed shut with no more noise than a tissue floating down onto a cushy pillow.

The Shiva's head's angle, the crazy height, and the brightness after the dark made Jericho's head swoon and he almost let go of the rail. "So *that's* what disconcerting means! I get it, get it, get it now!" Jericho said, trying not to throw up several pounds of wedding cake icing. He barely tasted it at the back of his throat. The icing had already boogied on down the digestive tract. This brought him to the realization that he had not eaten in several hours and a mild panic set in. He took a quick look at the Big Man and realized that *he* very obviously had never missed a meal. This gave Jericho a sense of peace and he quickly asked, "Say there Big Man, is there a, uh, kitchen on this tub?"

"How did you know my name?!" said the Big Man.

"Uh — what?"

"How did you know my name is Big Man?" he demanded.

"Lucky guess?"

THE SHIVA'S IMPRESSIVE LIBRARY

NATHAN WALKED into Shiva's library. The library was, well, *sumptuous*. Much like his 'bury your head in the sand fantasies' of the Oxford Bodleian Library, this caused him to completely relax. Though the ceiling was the same height as the rest of the ship, it was covered in dark wood paneling with beautifully made bookshelves that matched. The majority of the books were valuable leather editions, there were however a few paperbacks and professional journals mixed in. There were two large chairs of rich red velvet with brass buttons. Between them was a mahogany coffee table with pewter coffee service. The rich scent of the coffee made Nathan painfully aware of how bad he stunk. The woman took a few moments to sit, wincing as she did. She smiled when she found that comfy sweet spot. She motioned for Nathan to sit.

He looked from his human and alligator vomit-stained clothes to the velvet chair which seemed to be calling to him, *sit on me, please.* He paused, good manners holding his slothful beast side at bay.

"If you are concerned about the velvet, don't be," the woman said and leaned forward conspiratorially. "It's made of microfiber and cleans easily. It should be called miracle fiber in my opinion."

Nathan daintily tried his best not to put all his weight down but gravity had the last laugh and down he sat.

"Oooh, this is sooo comfortable!" Nathan said and couldn't help laughing.

"It really is. I wish I could run the whole ship from here, but, well, wishes aren't fishes," she said and leaned back, "You have questions. What are they?"

Nathan cleared his throat and said, "Why?"

A moment passed. The woman leaned forward and poured two coffees. She handed one to Nathan and smiled. She said, "I'm afraid you're going to have to narrow the scope of your question."

Nathan blinked and sputtered a bit of coffee onto his saucer.

She suppressed a smile and said, "I must apologize, you have had a shock and are taken aback. I'll tell you the story of why I am here and what exactly I am doing. Please feel free to interrupt me if I am not clear on any point. My name is Annabelle Lanier. You are far too young to know my father but he is, rather was — he's been dead for some time — a very wealthy man. I was sent to the best schools here and abroad. I had and still have, want for nothing. Contrary to what the newspapers had said at the time, my parents were not cold uncaring jet setters — our home exuded love. *However*, my father made his billions destroying rainforests, draining swamps, and — " Annabelle made 'quotation marks' with her fingers. "Being a *land developer*. Some would argue this is necessary. A needed thing. Nothing could be further from the truth. Take say, Los Angeles. Create a massive city *in the desert*. Then the citizens complain of droughts. They have created a city, yes, but it's still in the desert. Are they imbeciles, or has the heat baked their brains?"

"Nathan mixture of both, most likely," Nathan said.

Annabelle nodded and said, "The human condition in a nutshell. What concerns me is that the existing habitats — excuse me — *homes* for hundreds of thousands of animals are destroyed when jungles, swamps, and yes, bayous are drained and *developed*. Those animals don't relocate. They die as they are chased out of their home and are left to die. Or worse, are hunted for *sport*."

Nathan set his cup down and said, "So it is the Bayou Beast, sorry, the Shiva rather, that is being used to stop the drainage of this bayou."

"Exactly so. More space is not needed for people. They are being used because the swamps and 'waste lands' are even cheaper than run-down old neighborhoods and deserted factories. The land costs pennies and someone like my father is going to buy it. Then, hundreds of thousands of animals die so a family like mine can make even more money than we could spend for generations."

Nathan frowned, "Couldn't you simply buy up the land?"

"I could, but I am old and my nephews and nieces would cash in as soon as I am declared dead. No, the best tool is *fear*. I've made endless forests, jungles, and swamps no man's land through simple fear and more importantly, superstition. Superstition, though baseless, is good for generations. There are no ghosts. But how many people will go into an old basement with a flickering candle? Now blow that candle out. Fear becomes panic," Annabelle said and gave a wicked grin. "Fear is better than men with guns." She wrinkled her nose. "But, let's get you cleaned up and in a nice clean Gi."

"A martial arts Gi?" Nathan said and raised his eyebrows.

"Wash them repeatedly and they become oh so soft. And they are incredibly roomy. You'll see," Annabelle said and slowly got up.

THE SHIVA'S EVEN MORE
IMPRESSIVE GALLEY

THE BIG MAN was busy hustling over a range top, both hands flurrying about. One stirring, the other grabbing fresh herbs and splashing aromatic oils into the huge skillet there. His nostrils flared and he fought the urge to eat directly out of the hot pan. Hunger in the Big Man is strong however, and he soon burned his piggies trying to pluck tasty tidbits from the heavy black iron skillet. He jammed his burnt fingers in his mouth and sucked the savory sauce off them. He turned the flame even higher, the sizzling vegetables and tofu dancing in the surging heat. His eyes widened and he laughed maniacally, stirring faster and faster.

Jericho, freshly showered, scrubbed, and in a matching Gi, kept trying to get near the pan, wiping his drooling mouth repeatedly. When he came too close, the Big Man tossed some cooking sherry on the hot pan. A tremendous flame would blaze outward and quickly disappear — hibachi style — and hold Jericho at bay, his hairy lower brain chiding him, *Go easy man!*

Hunger in Jericho is also strong — strong like the Korean Ox is strong — but not nearly as smart as a Korean Ox. He soon lost an eyebrow to the flame. He daubed the ash away with his drool-soaked sleeve. His left leg was jiggling and he was about to start baying like a wolf when Annabelle and Nathan appeared in the hatchway. He turned and held out the sooty sleeve to them and said in a guttural voice, "*Fire — bad!*"

"What is happening in my galley?!" Annabelle said looking down to Jericho hunkered down by Big Man's side, "He hasn't — "

The Big Man laughed, his face red and dancing in the shadow of the flames. He said, "No Captain, not like you-know-who. He is very excited by the thought of this meal. Real excited."

Annabelle turned to Nathan and said, "When was the last time you two ate?!"

A vision passed through Nathan's mind of them eating enough wedding cake icing to kill a wooly mammoth not three hours ago. He looked to the flaming skillet and unconsciously made a spooning gesture with his hand and mumbled, "Well, when you are on a case time can get away from you and, um, whatnot, uh — *gosh, that smells fabulous.*"

"Perhaps you two should eat first, and then you will both be making more sense," Annabelle said. Before she could finish motioning to the table the brothers Kavillehogg had dashed over and sat bolt upright and were rubbing the tops of their thighs fast enough to light firewood. Annabelle brought two stainless steel cafeteria trays over to the range top. A final big splash of sherry created a miniature atomic mushroom cloud in the galley. The brothers clapped excitedly. The Big Man raised a hand to his chest and bent imperceptibly to his small but enthusiastic audience. They clapped even faster. He dished out heaping amounts of the savory vegetable and tofu stir fry with brown sauce onto the prison-style metal food trays. The trays bent in the center but held.

The clapping had ended and when Annabelle turned to the brothers they held their forks and knives outstretched, heads bowed to the tray as if in supplication to a minor deity. Annabelle paused and said, "What have I let onboard our ship?"

"Two hungry men, let's feed them. I will eat with

them — as a show of camaraderie, of course," said the Big Man behind her, holding two trays piled high with enough combined stir fry to bury a Sherman Tank. He arched an eyebrow and said, "I would recommend, Captain, that I *slide it* to them." He came close to the brothers and their clashing knives and forks threw off great sparks as they tried to get at the food. He slid the trays from a minimum safe distance. The brothers fell upon the food.

Annabelle said, "I like to see men with good appetites, but this is *savagery*. Look at them!"

The Big Man nodded, beginning to eat even before he sat. Between very large mouthfuls said, "Captain, my cooking has this effect on people with mighty appetites. Isn't that right boys?!"

The Kavillehoggs banged the tabletop with their utensils like rioting prisoners and then continued to shovel the tasty stir fry down their cavernous gullets, grunting, and whinnying.

Annabelle backed to the hatchway and said above the racket, "I will return when you three have finished — *dining*."

The Kavillehoggs were completely unaware that anyone was speaking to them. The Big Man waved goodbye with his knife — his fork was busy hauling wads of food to his eagerly waiting yap.

A CALL TO ACTION!

LATER, Annabelle rushed into the galley as fast as she was able and then screeched to a stop. The Big Man was slumped against the wall, his mouth hanging open, a stray noodle hanging there. The brothers were on either side of him, leaning against his massive belly. All three were snoring with a sound like gas generators, badly out of tune. The sheer volume of their snoring caused their metal food trays to rattle. The trays were so clean that they appeared to be polished.

She gently rubbed her hip. She then took a long spatula and gently poked the Big Man. "Wake up gentlemen, things are about to get exciting here," she said in an even tone. No response. She went to the refrigerator and pulled out a bottle of 'Stark Raving

Mad Eddy's Super-Duper Cola' and pried off the cap. She then wafted this under their collective noses.

The effect on Jericho was electric. He leapt up and over the table, snatched the bottle from Annabelle, and sucked on the bottle so hard that it shattered. Annabelle was truly awed that clean glass fell to the floor — Jericho had vacuumed up all of the sweet, sweet brown soda. She briefly thought of how happy Eddy would be to know that his product was so loved even after all these years. She removed herself from this revelry and said, "Young man, wake your gastronomic compadres and have them report to the bridge. And quickly please. I believe we are about to be boarded."

"Someone is gonna nail planks of wood on the Shiva?" Jericho said.

Annabelle briefly touched her temple and said, "Its a manner of speech meaning that someone is going to enter the ship. The end result will probably have us being put in prison for the remainder of our lives."

Jericho stared at her and said earnestly, "I don't want to go to jail. I heard the food is terrible."

Annabelle patted him gently, turned, and left the galley.

Jericho had broken a sweat and said to no one in particular, "And they only give you like, *sensible portions!*" He pulled the table away from his snoozing companions, jarring them awake. He shrieked, "I CAN'T LIVE ON 'SENSIBLE PORTIONS'!"

His compatriots leapt up and consoled him.

A POW WOW ON THE BRIDGE

THE THREE STUFFED men waddled onto the bridge of the Shiva. The bridge was very simple. A very large high-definition video screen covered each wall. This gave the impression of being able to 'see' all around the outside of the Shiva. A comfy executive swivel chair with a wireless keyboard across the lap area was at the center of the room. It also had two very cool-looking fighter jet joystick-style video game controllers on each armrest. Nathan was immediately jealous. He had his hands unconsciously came upright and made video gaming motions.

"What's the rumpus Captain?" Big Man said, coming up next to her.

Annabelle was hunched down tapping on the

keyboard. A satellite image of a C-130 which was very, very, very high over the area of the bayou popped up on the front screen. She was clearly flummoxed. She said, "It would appear someone is willing to make a HALO jump from 30,000 feet into a heavily wooded, alligator-populated bayou. What fool would attempt that?"

30,000 FEET ABOVE THE SHIVA

THE BETTY HELD One-Armed Bob at gunpoint.

She hollered through her respirator, "Jump out of the plane! What's wrong with you? You were a Ranger, right?!"

One-Armed Bob was buffeted by the turbulence at the downward-sloping, open cargo ramp of the C-130. He held onto the hydraulic lift with his real hand. All he could see were itsy-bitsy clouds *far beneath* them. When he left the US Army Rangers, the highest they ever jumped out of the planes was so low that it had allowed them to read the billboards lining the streets below. And the last billboard he saw from a jump was for a highly carcinogenic diet soda that tasted like grapefruit. With the exception of a good chance of getting cancer, he sure missed that brand.

He pulled his respirator away from his mouth and yelled, "There is NO reason to be jumping from this altitude. There are Cypress trees in the bayou. We're going to get tangled up in them and eaten by mosquitos or, with luck by an alligator." He hurriedly put his respirator back on, took a lungful of air and said, "This is stupid!"

The Betty turned crimson and yelled, "You callin' me stupid?"

With her free hand, The Betty took out a small sewing pin and let go of it. The howling of the turboprop engines and everything else died down to nothing. The flight crew and One-Armed Bob heard the pin drop. The noise resumed full blast.

The flight crew behind The Betty backed away some kind of quick. One actually sat down and covered his eyes.

One-Armed Bob has a long-term relationship with a no-nonsense intelligent woman. He realized he had crossed a line from which there was no return. The Betty leveled her gun at One-Armed Bob. He closed his eyes.

The Betty quickly holstered her gun, ran across the deck of the plane and took a flying tackle at One-

Armed Bob. The military plane kept moving forward but The Betty and One-Armed Bob stayed in the same place. Suddenly they were both falling toward the Earth with nothing but 30,000 feet of air between them and the bayou.

THE BETTY VERSUS GRAVITY: THE BETTY 1, GRAVITY 0

THE BETTY and One-Armed Bob were plummeting toward the Earth, now 28,000 feet between them and certain death, or at best, burlap sacks full of hurt.

The Betty was shaking One-Armed Bob, and was beginning to get frustrated.

"Wake up you tubby metal man!" she yelled and was about to smack him a good one when the *Iron Fist of Had Enough* shot up by itself and clamped onto her wrist. She winced and immediately stopped all attempts to wake him.

Then, *Iron Fist of Gentle Waking* let loose of The Betty and oh-so-gently shook One-Armed Bob's chin. His eyes opened slowly and he licked his lips.

He quickly realized where he was and his legs and arms shot straight out, clambering for anything solid.

"Whaaat?! Oh man, how high are we?" Bob demanded through his respirator.

The Betty checked the cluster of instruments strapped to her forearm and said, "Around 26,000 feet. Now we gotta come up with a plan. And pronto, we got about four minutes."

"You don't have a plan? What?!" Bob said unbelievingly. Even the iron fist looked startled.

The *Iron Fist of Utter Disbelief* turned to The Betty. She shrugged and said to it, "Look, all we gotta do is find the Beast, kill it, hack it open, and pull 'em out." She somehow managed to seem smug even during free fall.

The *Iron Fist of Complete and Utter Disbelief* now turned to One-Armed Bob. He shrugged energetically. As energetically as one can as one falls toward the Earth at thirty-three feet a second per second. He closed his eyes and tried to do the math as to how fast they would smack the ground if the parachutes failed to open. Bob was unable to do mental calculations while plummeting and gave up, deciding that the answer 'super-duper fast' was good enough. The *Iron Fist of Can You Believe This?* tapped him, jostling him from his fog of mental mathematics. Bob looked to his metal friend who in turn pointed to The Betty. Bob's mouth fell open in his respirator.

The Betty was having a one-woman muscular pose down. She was slowly rotating in midair as she popped a double bicep pose and then a double tricep extension. She then extended her legs and arms in a swimmer's pose, something impossible on land.

Bob was both impressed and hypnotized as she continued to throw out different poses in such a fluid and graceful manner from a woman who seemed about as graceful as a rusty fireplug. The Betty finished with a 'most muscular' pose as she and One-Armed Bob dropped through a flock of understandably surprised Herons. And then they were gone.

THE HERONS FLEW ON, languidly flapping their wings, glancing down at the falling humans. As a flock, they sighed and shook their heads in unison.

BATTLE STATIONS! OF SORTS...

IN THE CONTROL room of the Shiva, three uncomfortably stuffed men were bumping into each other and getting worked up.

Annabelle was working the joysticks of the control chair, looking up to the forward big hi-def screen. Fourteen submenus down and in a ludicrously small font were the tiny words 'battle stations' with an icon of a blunderbuss — an 1800s-style flintlock musket with a muzzle like a big black funnel. Annabelle looked to the men, cleared her throat, and said, "This one, gentlemen?"

All three ran up to the wall-mounted screen and scoured down through the maze of submenus. Jericho was the first to find the itty bitty blunderbuss and started flapping his arms about and said, "Yes! That's it! Push it, push it!"

Annabelle squinted at it and mused, "Do you think it will do any good?"

"YES!" the three men caterwauled.

Jericho ran over to where a giant speaker was mounted in the ceiling and girded himself for the alert.

Annabelle sighed and clicked on it. There was a low pathetic warble from the enormous overhead speaker and then the voice of a very young girl said, "Alert, alert," and then snickered. The warbling sound petered out and stopped.

Jericho, still fully girded, looked in a manly way to the giant speaker. He waited. Nothing else came. He said, "That's it? That's all? Man, I was all worked up!" He ungirded himself and slumped, clearly disappointed.

Annabelle smiled gently and said, "Young man, this system was designed by a young environmentalist who is also a Buddhist." She motioned to the submenus. "And quite literally, battle stations was at the bottom of his list." She slowly eased herself out of the captain's chair. "We will not fight, is that clear? We may defend ourselves, but without causing harm to others. More than likely, and considering that this is a halo insertion it will be members of our own armed forces. As the aliens on television enjoy saying, resistance would be futile — if not stupid. Or something along that line of thinking. I'm afraid we don't have time for much TV while saving the natural world. Do you think we should bring a white flag, or do they shoot at anything that moves?"

"We will go down with the ship!" Jericho said, his fist held high in the air. Big Man and Nathan slowly moved away from him, their eyes widening.

"Young man, I do believe you are caught up in the moment," Annabelle said and patted him on the shoulder. "But it is appreciated. You, however, are our guests — in an odd and amusing way. Myself and Big Man have sworn to stop the destruction of all remaining natural habitats and protect all those defenseless animals. You are here to, um... What exactly *are* you here for?"

Nathan lowered Jericho's fist, stepped forward, and said, "We have been hired to find a Professor Portsmouth as he was last seen — " Nathan stopped mid-sentence because Big Man and Annabelle were looking at their own feet like scolded toddlers.

Nathan said, "Oh gosh, he isn't — "

Annabelle suddenly brightened and said, "Oh no. He was trying to pursue The Shiva, believing it to be a dinosaur or, a *Bayou Beast*. The size and menacing aspect worked really well on just about everyone, but it worked a little too well with the Professor. Though he did manage to shoot at us with a, what did you call it Big Man?"

"A Mini-Gun, ma'am."

"Yes. An amusing name, considering its size and seeing that it sounds like the Apocalypse. It dented our hull considerably. After Shiva *ate* the Professor, well, he had a breakdown of sorts. He is alive, well fed, but — walking on his hands," Annabelle said and pursed her lips. "If you recall, fear and superstition is the main mission of the Shiva. It worked like gangbusters with the Professor."

"Gosh Nathan, that fancy pants marine scientist's convention isn't going to like this one tiny bit, are they?" Jericho said.

Nathan was thinking *exactly* the same thing, which bothered him greatly. Not the notion of upsetting the marine scientists — with or without fancy pants — but rather that he was capable of having the same thoughts as his brother. He shuddered.

"May we see the Professor? Before the Green Berets arrive?" Nathan said.

"We only have a few minutes, but of course," Annabelle said and led the way out of the control room. "I understand the special forces can land their parachutes with the precision of a surgeon."

A DISTINCTLY UNSURGICAL
LANDING

THE BETTY and One-Armed Bob were hanging, facedown, several inches above the snapping jaws of several bored and irritated alligators.

THE ALLIGATORS WERE IRKED because they were settling down after a great meal and had just got nice and comfy in the mud. The sun was warming them and life was spankin' good. Suddenly, these two clowns fall out of the sky — literally — and now their nap was good and ruined. But, scaring the stew out of humans was terrific sport and always made for great stories and gossip during those interminable months of hibernation.

Between snapping their jaws at them they would hiss really loud, which they rarely did when humans weren't around. It was so undignified. Then, something really gossip worthy happened. Antonio, a twenty-four-footer, miscalculated and snapped a little too high and bit the man's hand with a loud CLANG! Antonio broke several teeth, and worse, they knew how Tony would later gripe about it endlessly from now on. Regardless of the sheer amount of Tony's future whining, everyone cleared out, lickity split.

"WOULD you mind using your muscles to pull yourself upright up and cut me down?" One-Armed Bob said resignedly.

"I will!" The Betty said and using her hands scrambled up Bob's torso, stopped at his feet, and felt around her belt for a knife — which she did not bring. She would not admit this as the mission had been something of a disaster up to this point. She got close to the parachute cords, bunched them together and bit clean through them with a single snap of her perfect teeth, though stained a pretty tan color from her insanely strong coffee. She was smiling at her handiwork when she realized Bob was no longer there.

Gravity had done its bit and Bob had landed facedown into the mucky-muck up to his waist.

She swore she could hear his exposed boots sigh with exasperation. The Betty did an effortless sit-up, bit through her own lines and landed upright in the muck to her waist. She quickly snatched One-Armed Bob's ankles like an unhinged midwife and yanked him from the slimy mud. She then effortlessly tossed him to the firm grassy shore of the bayou.

He dazedly sat upright and expelled a huge wad of brown slime from his mouth. He stood and unhurriedly held out a hand to help her out of the mud. They were nine feet apart. He leaned over a few inches closer, and wasn't going to move even a bit more.

The Betty shimmied her way up and out of the mud, leapt next to One-Armed Bob, and jammed her muscular hands onto her muscular hips. They looked like a poor man's ying-yang symbol, One-Armed Bob smeared with brown slime from the waist up, The Betty from the waist down.

One-Armed Bob said nothing as he picked broken alligator teeth from the joints of the *Iron Fist of Filth*. He turned and handed the jagged broken teeth to The Betty. He wiped his eyes and then blew brown goop bubbles out his nostrils.

The Betty knew she had made one, well, *many* tactical errors. But here in the field, she was completely in her element. In charge. She told herself, *I am in control, total control!*

"Let's go get that Bayou Beast. I got a score to settle. Should be pretty close now. That pilot was circling over what she said was a big ol' reading. Let's go!" she said and looked left and right and left again. To the left seemed good, real good. She started stomping off in that direction. "This way! I'm gonna kill that thing soooo dead! We're gonna have Beast steaks for breakfast, lunch, and dinner. The size of, of, manhole covers!"

The Betty had covered a good seventeen feet when she noticed One-Armed Bob hadn't moved. She slapped her muddy thigh like one would call a dog over and said, "Come on, let's go!"

Bob refused to be brought to heel or be fetched.

"What's the problem? Why aren't you obeying?!" The Betty said and slapped her thigh again.

He tried not to laugh at her hissy fit. He pointed behind her across the winding bayou.

Towering above the cypress trees was an enormous hammer-headed monster. The Betty's eyes tried their best to pop out of her head and were restrained only by the overdeveloped muscles behind them. By sheer instinct and much practice, she grabbed for her gigantic pistol. It wasn't there. She returned her hand and grabbed at the empty holster over and over for a total of five times. She looked down and momentarily freaked, spun in a tight circle but quickly regained her composure. Her hands rose before her eyes. She nodded to them as if they had spoken to her.

She turned and glared at the Beast. In her mind it was staring right at her, taunting her. She raised a fist and shook it at the unmoving Beast saying, "I gotta bone to pick with you!" She marched directly off the shore and into the bayou, where she promptly disappeared under the water. Air bubbles broke the water's surface in a straight line. Fish and snakes leapt out of the water a few feet ahead of the air bubbles. Then the bubbles stopped. A few moments passed.

One-Armed Bob started to worry and walked to the edge of the shore. Her still-shaking fist broke the surface of the water near the opposite bank. She continued to march up and out of the water as if it were nothing. She turned and impatiently waved for Bob to come over. He did not budge.

He had only met this firebrand of a woman an hour ago. She and some tired guard with several holes in his bulletproof vest marched into his surplus store. But, her badge was real and when she said that an airboat captain called her on his museum-piece cellular phone, well, he couldn't refuse to help. Those boys were out here and he sensed they were in trouble. He had always felt that guns and unnecessary force were the way to go, but this lady brought all that to a new level. The air quivered as she walked through it. People like that got through wars without so much as a scratch. However, people around them tended to end up in cemeteries.

"What's your plan? And your contingencies plan if things go wrong?" he said.

You could heard the cogs turning in her head, looking for the words 'plan' or 'contingency.' One-Armed Bob waited for the cogs to stop.

A small bell, like one in a typewriter, pinged in her head. "We kill the Bayou Beast, climb down its throat and pull them boys out," she said and smirked, as if Bob were a rank amateur and never did this sort of thing.

"You said that before. *With what* do we kill the beast? Snarky smirks like that?" Bob shot back.

The Betty was about to march back and feed those words to Bob when she remembered, "Oh hey, I've got my backup to my backup pistol!" She rummaged around the waistband at the back of her fatigue pants. She pulled out a pitiful little automatic pistol and said, "Can't wear it in the front you know, my abs — no space!"

One-Armed Bob pointed to the absolutely still head of the Beast which appeared to taunt them from high over the tree line. He said, "I don't think we can even get its attention with that thing, much less kill it with your, um, *pistol*."

"I can light a match from a hundred feet away with this *pistol*," she said and pointed at the gun as if that proved her point.

"Perhaps that need will pop up," One-Armed Bob sighed, knowing that arguing with this federal agent was a total waste of time. He slowly trudged across the bayou, holding his iron hand above the water's surface to help prevent rust.

THE PROFESSOR'S... KENNEL

ANNABELLE OPENED the door to a well-lit but smallish room. Classical music played from a tiny speaker in the ceiling. Nathan was clearing the doorway thinking that *he* would like to stay in this comfy room and —

"High Tailin' Jiminy!" Nathan uttered and stopped dead, one foot staying midair above the floor. In the corner was, well, a kennel. And the guy in it he *sincerely hoped* was not the Professor.

The man in the kennel was in a Gi, but its sash was hanging in his face because he was 'walking' about in a handstand muttering, "Woof, woof." He was clearly deranged but seemed at the same time to be very happy. He would stop every few hand steps, lick his forearm and then rub his face with it. There were several newspapers spread out under him. He stopped and licked at a big upside-down hamster-style water bottle.

Annabelle was shuffling her feet and inspecting the ceiling as if it were completely fascinating. She said, offhandedly, "He truly enjoys catchy music. He will hum Saber Dance several times a day. He will clap excitedly with his feet when it plays. We only play it so much though because that sort of thing will drive you crazy — um, well — you understand. One can only hear Khachaturian so many times. He leans against the enclosure when he —"

"Kennel. He's in a kennel," Nathan said, exasperated. "He's acting like a dog — a dog doing a really good handstand."

"True, but we've only had him two days," Annabelle said, brightening. "We hope to have him on all fours soon."

"Ma'am, just drop us off anywhere and we can get him proper help. We need to get moving before the Marines or whoever will be here and — " Nathan was cut off by a loud ping from the overhead speaker.

"Captain, there are two people approaching the starboard side of the Shiva," Big Man said over the speaker.

The Professor started to growl at the speaker.

Nathan stepped back and reflexively held his hands up to his chest so as not to get bitten. Not taking his eyes off the upside-down Professor, he said, "Why is he growling?"

"Oh, he won't bite. He's being fussy because the music stopped," Annabelle said. She leaned forward and said quietly, "In addition, Big Man refuses to take him for walks, to potty, you realize. He insists that the Professor is already house-trained, in a manner of speaking, and takes him with a leash to the bathroom. Well, this naughty Professor intentionally peed on the floor *right next to the potty*. Rightfully, in my opinion, Big Man rubbed the Professor's face in it and popped him on the nose with a rolled newspaper. I've never had a dog, so I really don't know what the protocol is for that situation." She shrugged as if to say, *dogs — what can you do?*

Nathan decided that he wanted off this ship, pronto. He said, "Perhaps we could bring him with us to the control room? Regardless of what the authorities decide, he needs help in a proper facility. Perhaps a place with trees and a good fire hydrant."

The Professor started to shimmy his hips excitedly and panted.

Nathan started for the kennel and was handed a makeshift leash by Annabelle. He stared at it.

"Trust me. When he gets away from you it is the dickens to get catch him, he's a little scamp," she said, shook a finger at the Professor, and left the room. From the hallway she said, "You will find us up in the 'head' of the Shiva. We need to get our guests on the ship before the Navy or Army or whoever descends on us. Don't want them taking potshots at the wrong people. I have had several experiences of being shot at. Those military types can get very trigger-happy."

Nathan walked closer to the kennel and the Professor bared his teeth.

"Easy boy! Um, Professor," Nathan said as the Professor bit at the kennel bars. Nathan reflexively whipped the bars with the leash. "Down boy, I say, heel!"

The Professor whimpered and backed away. Nathan immediately felt awful and crouched down low. He said, in a happy-wappy baby voice, "How'd you like to go for a walk, *outside*?"

The Professor leapt up and down on his hands and said, "Woof!"

MEANWHILE, OUTSIDE THE SHIVA

THE BETTY KICKED the Shiva one more time for good measure. The steel was so thick it didn't even make a thump. She pulled out her diminutive pistol and was about to squeeze off a round when, deep in her brain, her Good Judgement came out of retirement and cleared its throat. The Betty straightened up and her eyes rolled back in her head.

GOOD JUDGEMENT SAID, "I have been quiet ever since that big bully the Id, beat the stuffing out of me for even mentioning that plunging off a cliff into a forest fire driving a gasoline tanker was a *poor idea*. However, even a peacenik like myself can unabashedly say that this Bayou Beast thing is made out of heavy gauge armor. That empty Mini-Gun over there only chipped the paint up a bit. Ergo, our admittedly accurate, but small caliber pistol is not the weapon of choice. Kicking said Beast is only going to get us dragging a broken foot through a dangerous bayou. And for what? So you could kick it? Here is a proposal — take the Mini-Gun and use it to knock on the metal. Get them to let us inside and, when inside, produce the pea shooter to make demands."

THE BETTY'S eyes rolled back to the front. Her brain, a seething, bubbling mess was about to actually listen to Good Judgement for the first time in years. Unfortunately, One-Armed Bob chose that moment to jump down from an airboat close by that was sticking upright in the mud. He was now wearing a backpack with funny writing on the back. He turned and was holding what looked, to The Betty, like the most awesome pig sticker made — *ever*.

THE BETTY'S crackling brain went into overdrive and rattled around in her skull. Neurons were firing off so fast that they were arcing from one side of the brain all the way to the other. The Id, who had snuck up behind Good Judgement, had spun it around and socked it a good one on the jaw. Good Judgment dropped like a fifty-pound sack of rice. The Id then dragged Good Judgement way, way into the back of the brain and into a storage closet behind all the unused cleaning supplies. The Id threw the key over its shoulder and guffawed, knowing no one has *ever* gone in there. The Id ran back to the Conscious where all the fun was happening. The Ego gave the Id a high five and then head-butted it for — heck, it didn't *need* a reason. *It just felt good doing it.*

ONE-ARMED BOB, for the first time since being tackled out of the cargo hold of an airplane, felt at home. He rubbed the giant shiny harpoon barb of the Arm of Zeus. He winced a bit, drew back his thumb, and stuck it in his mouth. That barb could be used for shaving in a pinch.

"If we poke a hole below the waterline, that

should create all sorts of craziness on board," One-Armed Bob said.

"Won't it sink it?" The Betty demanded, returning her itsy-bitsy pistol to its hiding place.

One-Armed Bob laughed, gestured to the Beast and said, "Miss, this thing is so huge that it is most likely, no, *it is* resting on the bottom. I would bet it travels on caterpillar tracks like a tank. Hey, I bet if I were to shoot it in its head — "

A shadow had passed over them. As they looked up the open mouth of the Shiva fell down over them, its hundreds of teeth engulfing them.

———

IN THE DUSTY storage closet in The Betty's brain, from behind a locked door a voice muttered, "I tell you and I tell you and I tell you. But you just won't listen."

No one responded however, because no one was listening.

IN THE MOUTH OF THE SHIVA

ONE-ARMED BOB WAS on the floor shrieking.

The Betty was rolling around hollering.

The Kavillehoggs were aghast.

The Professor was barking like crazy, yanking at his leash.

Big Man and Annabelle had hands on hips, shaking their heads in dismay.

One-Armed Bob regained his dignity first. He stood up and brushed himself off, acting as if nothing had happened. However, the Arm of Zeus backpack was all wonky on his back making him look as if he were a low-rent bug exterminator. He reached over and tapped The Betty's shoe with the barb of the harpoon and she stopped hollering.

She briskly shook her hair free of mud like a

collie on amphetamines. Then, from a laying position, she jerked herself upright and simultaneously produced her small automatic pistol.

It was like a very good magic act and everyone politely clapped as if at a tennis match. The Professor excitedly barked once.

"YOU MAKIN' FUN OF ME!?" The Betty yelled so loud that the Professor yipped once and curled into a ball.

"Young lady," Annabelle said and moved between The Betty and everyone in the line of fire, "None of us are armed."

"*I am*," The Betty beamed.

Annabelle pursed her lips and said, "That is certainly true. I was wrong and you are right. That appears to be a very nice pistol." She turned to Big Man and raised an eyebrow and said, "Don't you think it is?"

He nodded, turned to The Betty and said, "I do. Back when *I* used to hurt people, that was one of my favorites. Easily concealed, little kick and could light a match from fifty feet."

"One hundred," The Betty winked and crinkled her muddy nose to Big Man, who smiled easily at her. She smiled back.

Annabelle looked to the ceiling and closed her

eyes. She said, "My goodness. Well, you certainly don't need it with us, as there are no weapons on board the Shiva."

"There's one now, honey," The Betty said and waved the pistol nonchalantly, not taking her eyes off Big Man.

"Are you a member of the armed forces?" Annabelle said. This got The Betty's attention. She pried her eyes away from Big Man.

"Betty Catskill, Special Agent, Federal Bureau of Investigation," The Betty said and puffed herself up a bit as she did.

"Question. How did you get the military to place you in a halo drop?" Annabelle said and crossed her arms.

"I told 'em to. I swear those guys are all 'permission this, gotta have orders that.' It makes you crazy!" The Betty said, punctuating with her gun in the air.

"Not the answer I was expecting. I do enjoy hearing about other women making their way in a world still run mostly by men," Annabelle said.

"Got that right!" The Betty said, hands on hips.

"Well, I am fresh out of questions," Annabelle said and brought her wrists forward, "we are your prisoners. Please be gentle as my joints are quite arthritic."

The Betty had never had anyone simply *give up*. *And so nicely*. This was completely out of her experience, training, and anything she had ever seen on television. It made her adrenal gland squirt out a good half cup of go-go juice into her bloodstream. This, injected into a body that was always going full steam ahead made her squeeze off a shot at the first thing that moved. Unfortunately for Big Man, it was him. In one of life's weird ironies, he was taking his hand off the big red lever so as not to drop her eighty feet to the ground as he did the airboat hours ago. It was that forearm that she shot.

Everyone jumped including the Professor who leapt upside-down up and at The Betty. He pinned her down and bit her wrist making her drop the gun. One-Armed Bob grabbed and crushed the gun with the *Iron Fist Of Had Just About Enough Of This*.

Everyone looked to the Big Man. He grabbed his wrist just below the bullet hole and squeezed. He continued this milking motion up his arm up to the armpit. He then squeezed his shoulder and worked his way to his neck. By now The Betty was inches from him, pure-d-fascinated at this show of strength and mastery over pain. Big Man squeezed his neck twice, produced the bullet between his teeth, and gently blew it out at her. It bounced off her forehead and clinked on the steel floor.

"Tell me you 'ain't married," The Betty said.

"I am not. And from one professional to another, thank you for hitting me in the muscle and not in an artery," Big Man said.

The Betty grabbed a roll of duct tape and, peeling off a length, bit it off and stuck it over the bullet hole. She tipped her head coyly and said, "I'm not a killer, Big Man."

"How did you know my name?"

Everyone looked to The Betty, even the upside-down Professor, who was rubbing his head against Annabelle's ankle.

The Betty reached out and gave Big Man's massive bicep a good squeeze and said, "Well, if ain't that, *it should be.*"

THE FINAL INTERLUDE

NATHAN OPENED a letter and pulled out an invoice that was uncharacteristically written all in capital letters with exclamation points placed every few words. It was as if the person writing it was having some sort of fit, which, in fact, they had. He handed this to Jericho who looked to the final figure at the bottom of the invoice which was, oddly, written with a...

"I think this whole ruined truck thing has affected Ariolano. I mean. Look how big he wrote that total. And with a *red crayon* no less," Jericho said and added that figure to a long tally on a notepad nestled between several bags and many empty chocolate truffle wrappers. He blew at the wrappers and created a small storm, sending them everywhere.

Nathan shuffled the wrappers about, looking for any more unopened envelopes. He stopped when he realized that there were simply too many wrappers. He did the traditional Kavillehogg thing and gave up. Perhaps an enterprising archeologist would someday find any receipts he hadn't opened. Nathan was pleased with that thought. The Howard Carter's of the world needed work too.

The microwave pinged behind him. Glad of the distraction, he turned and banged his leg. He managed to get the bowl out of the microwave and almost dropped it. Jericho let out a gasp.

"I got this, big brother. As if a Kavillehogg would drop three and a half pounds of melted truffles! Bring on the straws of eternal life!" Nathan placed the bowl between him and Jericho.

Jericho threw a turkey baster to Nathan and kept one for himself. They looked each other in the eye and nodded, the race officially on.

Each ripped the rubber baster bulb off and jammed the big long plastic tubes into the bowl of bubbling melted awesomeness. The sucking gurgling sound was both frightening and exhilarating. They were almost to the bottom of the bowl when Jericho looked up at Nathan and started snickering. This in turn caused him to blow, instead of suck into his turkey baster. This of course created a huge chocolate air bubble. The cohesive force of melted truffles is, to say the least, weak. The giant bubble burst and covered them both with yummy chocolate and rice crispies. Both were surprised and at the same time disappointed that the chocolate was *on* them, and not *in* them.

The shed doors were jerked open. Both turned to the blazing light and hissed like geese. The sight of the Kavillehogg's teeth, coated with a thick layer of melted truffles, would have put a dentist in a straight jacket. They squinted at the light and threw their arms across their eyes like vampires.

"I still can't believe you two solved this case in under a day. I mean, really. Last time I saw you two you were being force-fed with a shovel by a woman who was huffing a steel tray so heavy with food that it was *bending*," Jaqueline Portsmouth said as she crossed the threshold.

"Huh?" Nathan said, his brain still coping with the pound and a half of sugar racing through it.

Jericho was making a zip-your-lip motion to Jaqueline as he grabbed for her one of those 'folds up into four poles' beach sling chairs. She grudgingly nodded an oath of silence to Jericho. She turned to Nathan and said, "Perhaps I saw that on the television," and then faced Jericho. "Or maybe a bad dream."

"Probably both," Jericho said, nodding.

Jaqueline tried to make herself comfortable in a chair designed to deny comfort, no matter how you sat in it. She gave up and said, "I thought you two would like to know the results of your — *adventure.* First off, those two from the swamp machine were not even brought to trial. Apparently, the FBI person didn't have a warrant, shanghaied an Army C-130, and then fired on unarmed people who had clearly given up to her."

The brothers nodded.

Nathan said, "Yes, that pretty well encapsulated what she did. She did apologize to Big Man, though. I really don't think she intended to shoot him and —"

Jaqueline held up a hand and said, "Uh-huh. Heard she and Big Man are an item now. The Professor was brought to the conference and though he did some pretty neat tricks —catching a frisbee with his teeth as he jumped from table to table — his contribution was pretty well nil." She tried again to get comfortable in the Venus flytrap of a chair. Narrowing her eyes she stuck her hand down into the cup holder on the arm. It came out with the cleaned bone of a chicken leg. "Of all that is holy. Is this a —"

Nathan quickly took the bone away mumbling, "An experiment. Tell us more!"

"Experiment in complete and utter grossness," she countered.

Nathan piped up, "Surely not *utter*. What did happen? It is apparent no war broke out."

She collected her thoughts and said, "That's true. His madness *actually helped*. His fellow scientists confided to my boss that the Professor was something of a pain, you know where. They said not only did he 'shake hands' now he would even — if given a treat first of course — 'roll over and play dead' during the important meetings during the conference. Turned out to be his best behavior in years."

She shrugged as if to say, *self-aggrandizing scientists — what can you do?*

"It came out during our investigation that you are not his daughter," Nathan began.

"And that he isn't your dad!" Jericho piped up.

Both Jaqueline and Nathan closed their eyes.

"Okay, I work for the Secretary of State. I help solve problems. You have no idea how it pains me, but my boss wants to put you two — *detectives* — on an embarrassingly large retainer and be available to assist the country at a moment's notice. He said — I'm serious now — he actually said, 'America needs men like the Kavillehogg brothers.' I still can't believe my boss is so high up on the ladder. Anyway, we have a serious problem in Rome and we need you — "

Jericho held out two chocolate-stained hands and said, "Whoa, lady. We finally got our expenses and hours added up and put together and are fixing up a kinda bill, I guess we in the business we call it a — bill."

"How much?" she said and held out her hand making a 'come on' gesture with her long, well-manicured fingers.

Nathan wasn't about to look a gift horse in the mouth and rushed to put the tally list in her hand. She barely glanced at it and said, "Sure, fine."

The brothers looked at each other bug-eyed, trying not to scream.

Jaqueline gave them a blank check. She said, "You'll receive two unlimited credit cards in the mail." She looked about the shed. "Get a real office. And a car. Make it a super fast one, in this line of work you're going to need it."

She quite ungracefully got up from the deadly framed sling chair and stopped at the doorway and said, "Gents, don't *ever* put those kinds of figures down for *food* on an expense report. Someone who hasn't seen you two eat would *ever* believe those numbers. *I wouldn't* and I've seen your freak show in action. Always give them straight to me. Boys, I'll see you in Rome."

AFTERWORD

The James Bond films *used* to end with the title of the next 007 films. I fully intend to keep up the tradition. Nathan and Jericho Kavillehogg will return in...

The Starving Detectives Go To New Orleans